How to Not Fall for the Guy Next Door, Book One in the How to Not Fall series

Copyright © 2020, 2025 by Meg Easton

Interior Design by Mountain Heights Publishing

Author website: www.megeaston.com

Also by Meg Easton

Romancing the Spy romantic comedies

Spies Don't Fall for Their Asset

Spies Don't Fall for Their Rival

Spies Don't Fall for Their Neighbor (coming 2025)

Spiced Chais and Secret Spies

Holiday Lights & Cocoa Cookie Nights

––––––

How to Not Fall romantic comedies

How to Not Fall for the Guy Next Door

How to Not Fall for the Wrong Guy

How to Not Fall for Your Best Friend

How to Not Fall for Your Ex

––––––

A Mountain Springs Christmas

The Christmas Pact

The Christmas Bet

The Christmas Clause

––––––

Nestled Hollow Romance

Coming Home to the Top of Main Street

Second Chance on the Corner of Main Street

Christmas at the End of Main Street

More than Friends in the Middle of Main Street

Love Again at the Heart of Main Street

More than Enemies on the Bridge of Main Street

———

Love Started romances

It Started with a Sunset

It Started with a Note

It Started with a Glance

———

Silver Leaf Falls romance

Coming Home to Silver Leaf Falls

HOW TO NOT FALL for the GUY NEXT DOOR

HOW TO NOT FALL for the GUY NEXT DOOR

MEG EASTON

Contents

CHAPTER 1

Addison

I TURN my car into the parking lot of Gateway Groceries in Quicksand, Oregon, and then pull into a stall before calling my sister. Just like every time I've talked to her over the past three days, I can hear her concern just from the breath she takes in. Before she can even say, "Hello?" I say, "I didn't die."

Chloe squeals. "So you're home, then?"

Home. It feels weird to call Quicksand "home." I spent my summers from ages ten to thirteen here, but that hadn't made it "home" any more than playing Barbie Dreamhouse meant I was married to Ken. Amarillo is home. Quicksand was always temporary. An exciting game of dress-up. I wonder how long it'll take before calling this place *home* won't seem weird.

"I'm in Quicksand, but not at the inn. The moving truck is forty-five minutes behind me, so I'm stopping at the grocery store." My stomach is growling almost as loudly as my radio was playing, so getting food is essential.

Chloe lets out a relieved breath. "Oh, I'm so glad you made it safely."

"I told you I could make it sixteen hundred miles across six states on my own. See? You should leave the worrying to the older sister. I'm better at it anyway."

I grab my purse and get out of my car as my sister laughs. Then I take in a long, deep breath of air I haven't smelled in over thirteen years. It's fresh, like trees and rich soil, both of which are currently wet from a recent rainstorm. The air itself feels wet, actually. Maybe because there are so many trees here, all with moss-covered trunks. Trees and blackberry bushes.

I shake out my legs and stretch my back before I start walking toward the building. Spending twenty-five hours in a car, six of them this morning, really did a number on my muscles.

"Speaking of worrying," I say, "I still feel awful that I left a week before you move out of the freaking country. Do you need me to fly back to make sure you get off okay?"

"Nope. Dustin and I have everything under control. *You stay there.*" Each word is a punch. A hammer on a nail to hold me firmly in Quicksand. "I didn't make your website and ads for you to miss your first clients."

"You're so bossy."

I hear Chloe's grin through the phone. "I learned from the best. Now, go grab that fresh start by the horns and show it who's boss!"

"Yes, ma'am!"

"And then call me after the movers leave."

"I will."

I push the phone into my purse, take a deep breath, and walk through the automatic front doors of Gateway Groceries. Packing up everything I own, saying goodbye to the city where I've lived my entire life, leaving the sister I've never lived more than a five-minute drive from, and moving halfway across the country to a place where I know exactly zero people is fine. I am fine. Everything is fine.

Piece of cake.

As I wander aimlessly up and down the aisles with no plan, I realize I probably should've spent less time on the drive jamming out to the radio, playing the license plate game solo, and trying to distract myself from thoughts of Matthew, my old job, my hometown, and everything I left behind, and more time coming up with a grocery list. I have no idea what food is at the inn if there is anything at all. For the past four years, my Aunt Helen hadn't used the property as an inn—she lived there with her nurse like it was just a big house. And for the past three months since she passed away, no one has lived there at all.

So there could be things like spices, flour, sugar, coffee, and maybe even some food in the freezer. Or there could be nothing—I have no idea if anyone packed anything up at all. It's a mystery. And mysteries are fun, right? I mean, it's what I spent two years trying to convince Matthew of. This would probably drive him nuts, all the not knowing. But things between us are over, so I am going to relish every single mystery that he would've hated.

I change my mind about shopping for staples before

checking out the inn, and instead, I decide the best plan is to get some fresh fruits and vegetables and maybe soup I can easily warm up. With only a few things in my cart from my meandering trip through the store, I turn toward the produce area.

The deli faces the produce section, and as the older man behind the counter finishes up with a customer, he turns his attention my way, studying me. Against his olive skin, his white eyebrows stand out, looking rather judgy as they come together over his curious eyes. At a population of ten thousand, Quicksand isn't exactly small-town-ish enough for everyone to know everyone, so I must have an *I'm new here* look about me. Maybe he's trying to figure out if I am just visiting or putting down roots.

He has pretty keen eyes, too. Maybe he's seeing me deeply enough to notice that under the surface, I have a panicked *my life was recently planned out, perfect, and organized and is now a big mess of uncertainty and chaos* look about me.

I give him a little smile and shift my eyes to his case of hot food, hoping he'll do the same. My stomach rumbles again at seeing the food. It's been too many hours since I grabbed that muffin and orange juice from my hotel back in Boise. Maybe I should forget the microwaveable soup and go up to the man and get some fried chicken, or a burrito, or some potato wedges. It isn't what my body is begging me for, but it's something I can eat in the car on my way to the inn, and right now, my body is saying that the speed at which I get food in my belly matters.

After I get produce. I turn away from the warm, fried foods and aim my cart's trajectory toward the apples.

Before long, I have a cart full of enough fruits and vegetables of differing colors that my Aunt Helen would've been proud. They say you shouldn't go grocery shopping while hungry. But maybe going when you're ravenous after having just spent two and a half days in a car while eating nothing but junk food is the absolute best time to go if you want a cart full of healthy stuff.

The fruit aisle has a few other shoppers in it, so I leave my cart at the end of the aisle and make my way down it. Blueberries! That's exactly what my body needs. I pick up a few of the plastic cases, inspecting them closely to find the freshest ones. Two containers are perfect enough that my mouth starts watering. I have got to finish this shopping trip quickly so I can gobble up at least one of the containers. I spin toward my cart, a container of blueberries in each hand, and smack right into a man's very firm chest.

I yelp as we collide, and several nearby customers leap back as the flimsy plastic containers burst open, sending blueberries flying like soda from a shaken can, hitting the laminate floor with dozens of the softest pings, followed by the only slightly louder sounds of the two plastic containers making their landing on the floor.

"Oh no. I am so sorry." My face flames and I quickly brush at the bluish-purple spots that a few of the more aggressive blueberries left on the man's light blue t-shirt, as if a few swipes of my fingers will make the stains disappear.

"It's okay." The man gently moves my frantic hands away from his shirt. Probably because he's a little uncomfortable with having them all over his chest. "It's not a big deal. Really. I don't even like this shirt."

The man's voice is deep and rumbly, like summer thunder on the beach. I finally look up to meet his eyes and blush even more at seeing that his face is even nicer than his considerably nice chest. And his stunning blue eyes, which definitely look like his shirt should get a medal for what they do for them, aren't angry or irritated or frustrated—they are amused.

Amused is good. It isn't *good* good, but on a scale of one to thoroughly embarrassed at the grocery store, I'll take being the source of someone's amusement over being the source of someone's anger or frustration.

"Cleanup in produce," sounds over the intercom, and I look over at the very unimpressed man at the deli who now has one white eyebrow raised in an *I knew you'd be trouble* arc.

I force myself to breathe. Then I clear my throat and crouch, pick up one of the fallen plastic containers, and start putting blueberries back into it. The man crouches, too, which puts us in very close proximity especially since we can't exactly take a single step in any direction without squashing blueberries.

It takes several fast heartbeats before I steal another glance at him. I'd been so distracted by his eyes before that I hadn't noticed his beautifully strong jawline or the way that, when relaxed and in their natural state, the muscles of his face show that they spend a good portion of their time smiling.

And there's something about him that's familiar. I'm about to ask him if we've met before, but then a gangly teenage boy comes over with a broom and a dustpan and says he'll finish cleaning up the mess. As I carefully tiptoe away from ground zero and toward safety, I decide against asking the man. Mainly because I don't want to do anything else that might make me more memorable to him or anyone else right now. And besides, I know absolutely no one in this town, so just because he has a familiarity about him doesn't mean I know him.

The man steps to the edge of the fallen blueberries and reaches across the strawberries and blackberries to grab two more containers of blueberries. Then he hands them to me and says, "It looks like we both survived the Great Blueberry Explosion. Congratulations."

"You, too." I carefully add them to my cart so I don't accidentally bump one of the lids and make it pop open. "But I am sorry that we didn't all make it. If you would like me to say any words at the funeral of your shirt, let me know."

He chuckles. "Are you visiting?"

"Just moving in," I say, then in a panic, I glance at my watch. I somehow completely forgot that I don't have all the time in the world. "I've got to run. I'm supposed to meet the moving truck at the inn in ten minutes."

This time when he gives me that amused expression, I notice the smile that came with it. A smile that could melt the snow on Mount Hood. "I'll see you around, then."

"And next time," I call out as I hurry toward the checkout lines, "I promise not to be armed with blueberries."

I'm back in my car and trying to somehow magically get to the inn more quickly—without speeding—when the embarrassment hits me again. I wasn't even in my new city for thirty minutes before making a fool of myself. It isn't exactly the stellar start I'd been hoping for.

But embarrassing or not, I smile when I think back on how our interaction ended. Those last few comments I made could probably be considered flirting. I, Addison Sparks, had actually flirted with a very cute man. I am pretty proud of myself. Matthew and I had been together for more than two years, and we were long past our days of flirting with each other. And since our breakup, I've been mourning the loss of the future I thought I'd have with him, which made me not exactly feel like flirting. Honestly, I wasn't even sure I remembered how to flirt.

Today feels like progress. I kind of wish Matthew had witnessed it.

Not that I'm likely to ever again see the man I inadvertently attacked with blueberries. I went to my neighborhood grocery store back in Amarillo all the time for years, and I rarely bumped into people I knew, so I know that chances are small that I'll see him again. But it was nice flirting with him because it made me realize that one day I'll eventually want a relationship again, even if I don't want one now. And I'm glad the man will stay a stranger. I prefer first interactions to not involve ruining a man's shirt and then accidentally putting my hands all over his chest.

My face flushes again at the memory, so I try to focus on the road. I haven't stayed the summer at the inn with my aunt since I was thirteen, but I can still make my way to the inn on autopilot while scarfing down a protein bar that I picked up at the grocery checkout. And the scenery here easily grabs my attention. Amarillo doesn't have these tree-lined streets, and there's some bucket in me—I'm not sure what—that gets filled by driving in an area where the trees aren't just along the streets but seem to crowd in everywhere, only willing to pull back a bit for the homes and businesses around.

Coming to this place as a kid feels like a lifetime ago. So much so that during the two years Matthew and I dated, I never once told him about it. It feels weird to be in a place he knew nothing about. I wonder how he's doing back in his scheduled, predictable life while mine is in such new territory.

I somehow manage to arrive at the inn before the moving truck and pull into one of the eight spots in the small parking lot on the side, leaving the curving driveway in front open for the truck. After unlocking the front door, I walk back out to the edge of the road and stand next to the *Hidden Inn* sign so I can flag down the truck.

The sign that used to make my stomach leap in excitement as a girl now makes my heart palpitate and my muscles twitch. I wasn't at the reading of Aunt Helen's will, and I'd been unable to even form words when I first found out my aunt wanted me to have Hidden Inn. I added the inability to stand on my own two feet to the speechlessness once I found out my aunt said it was because "Addison will know what to do with it."

Some of my favorite childhood memories are of staying at the Hidden Inn, with my aunt treating me like I was an adult living in my own place. I spent many days there dreaming of the time when I'd be a strong, independent businesswoman in a power suit, living on my own.

I *never* dreamed of one day running the inn. Not even for a teeny tiny second. Why my aunt thought I'd know what to do with this place is beyond me. My parents were fairly absent when I was a kid, and the moment Chloe and I became adults, they moved to Florida. With their absence most of my life, I've craved family. And running an inn where I'd always be spending time with strangers doesn't sound appealing in the least. It wasn't until Chloe suggested that I run it as an apartment instead of as an inn that moving here felt right.

But *is* it right? Can a girl who's never lived more than five miles from her childhood home—and never more than two miles from her sister—make it in a new city by herself?

As I stand at the edge of the road, looking at the inn that I'm now responsible for, I'm not so sure. Yes, the building is paid for, but I've done the math, and for utilities, property taxes, taking care of the grounds, repairs, and a million other little costs that came to me one night at three a.m., I'll need roommates in at least three of the five bedrooms in the inn. Where am I going to find three roommates in a city where I know zero people?

My heart rate multiplies as I see the moving truck in the distance, lumbering its way toward me.

Then I remember reading that the only difference between nervousness and excitement is breathing. If you hold your breath, your body assumes you're nervous. If you breathe through it, it assumes excitement.

So I breathe. As the truck nears and then turns into the curved drive of the inn, the excitement builds.

And then the truck runs over one of the shrubs lining the

driveway, squashing it completely flat. The driver rolls down the window and calls toward me, "Sorry 'bout that!"

I breathe. Only excitement here. Nothing else to see.

I direct the movers to the three rooms my furniture and boxes need to go in—the kitchen with its big dining table and half a dozen breakfast tables, the gathering room that will be my family room, and my bedroom. The one Aunt Helen saved for me every summer for four years straight. The one that still makes me giddy as an adult every time I think of it. Then I head back outside to help bring in the boxes. I make it exactly one step from the house onto the wraparound porch before I freeze mid-step.

The man from the grocery store is standing near the back of the moving truck, wearing a dark gray shirt now, which is probably a smart choice if he's going to risk being around me and a moving truck. And, surprisingly, his eyes look even bluer than they did when he was wearing the blue shirt. Maybe it's just the Oregon sun working in his favor.

But what is he doing here? And how did he know this was where I was meeting the moving truck? The memory of smacking into him with the blueberries and sending them flying is admittedly a stronger memory than every little thing I might've said in my flustered state, but I'm pretty sure I didn't give him my address or any other location clues.

My shock at seeing him must last a second too long because that amused smile plays on his face again. He jumps out of the back of the truck, walks to the bottom of my porch stairs, and holds out his hand. I make myself remember how to use my legs again and walk forward, take the three steps down from my porch, and hold out my hand. He shakes it and says, "Hi again. Neighbor."

Neighbor? My eyes flash to the left—at the fancy wrought iron gate in the middle of a hedgerow that leads to a neighbor's house. And suddenly I realize why the man had looked familiar.

No, no, no. I can't be next-door neighbors with a guy I just embarrassed myself in front of at the grocery store. A guy who I was instantly attracted to, even while still getting over my ex.

And definitely not Ian Kendrick, the guy I had my very first crush on.

"You're looking good, Addi."

"Addison."

"What's it been? A dozen years?" He walks up the ramp of the moving truck, pausing to look back at what is surely a bewildered expression on my face.

"Thirteen. Did you recognize me at the grocery store?"

"Not until you said you had to meet the moving truck at the inn. Then I pieced it together." He disappears into the moving truck just as one of the movers comes out of my house.

I guess I did mention a location clue after all. "Why didn't you say anything?"

Ian emerges from the truck a moment later carrying one of my boxes and shrugs. "I thought this would be more fun."

I glance at the box he's holding. In the upper left corner, nicely printed on a label, are the words "Label collection." Yes, I like using labels. Yes, I like collecting labels. And not just labels—half the boxes filling the moving truck are empty organization containers of every size. Yes, I know from living in this world that most people think my obsession is weird. Ian already experienced blueberries with the adult version of his childhood friend. I don't need his second experience with me to be finding out this detail.

I'll just offer to take the box from him before he notices what it is. I rush down the stairs and toward the truck as he walks down the ramp with the box. My foot catches on the rock border at the edge of the curved driveway, and I lunge forward just as Ian steps off the side of the ramp, knocking us into each other.

Which, honestly, wouldn't be awful if he weren't holding the box. But the pressure of us crushing the cardboard box between us changes its shape just enough to pry the bottom flaps free from the packing tape and it flies open, dumping all of my labels of every size and shape, along with half a dozen different types of label makers, all over the driveway. And it happens just as one mover steps out of the truck and the other steps out of my house.

Ian and I both freeze, looking down at the contents of the box. Then he meets my eyes. "Do you always crush random containers between you and nearby men, or is it just me?"

"It's just you, Ian. Only you." Maybe I should just get in my trusty Camry and head back to Amarillo right now.

CHAPTER 2

Ian

I'VE SPENT the last several hours in the shop in my backyard, doing all the saw cuts, sanding, and pre-building I can on a massive built-in fireplace mantle, entertainment center, and bookshelves that will span an entire wall in the home I'm contracted to do the woodwork in.

As I run the piece across the belt sander, I look out the window and smile when I see Addi and one of her roommates talking in her backyard. She crouches down and runs her fingers across the top of the cut grass, seeming confused as to how it's freshly mowed when she hasn't done it. Sometime soon, I'll have to tell her that I'm still taking care of the inn's grounds, just like I did every summer growing up and like I've done for the last year and a half since I bought my grandparents' home.

I didn't actually recognize Addi when we had our rather explosive first meeting at the grocery store. It wasn't until she was at the registers that I placed where I'd last seen the adventurous gleam in her golden-green eyes or the familiar blush on her cheeks. She'd been pressing a flat rock into my palm that she'd painted with a scene of the two of us jumping into Quicksand River and telling me that she'd see me next summer. Then, while I was looking at the rock, she darted forward and kissed me on the cheek. It surprised me so much that I just stood there like an idiot who'd lost all ability to think or move.

And then she'd run off to get into her Aunt Helen's car, and they drove away to the airport. I was fourteen, so she must've been thirteen. I came back to spend the month of July with my grandparents the next summer, but she wasn't at the inn. Not that summer or any summer after.

I want to ask her about that and to catch up on where life has taken her in the past thirteen years. But when my now ex, Cara, stomped on my heart four weeks ago by calling off our wedding, she'd kind of stomped on my confidence, too, and now I'm questioning everything. So I've been keeping my distance from Addi, but because it's the right thing to do, I've still gone over to the inn to help every time I've seen one of her new roommates moving in during the past couple of weeks. I've discovered that I'm not the only one keeping my distance—Addi has pretty expertly avoided me every time, too.

I should probably just go tell Addi right now that I'm taking care of the yard because I doubt her aunt put it in writing anywhere. Yet, I hesitate. It's a busy season at work, so I have limited time to take care of the inn's grounds during daylight hours. But since Addi's avoiding me, part of me wants to see how long I can keep mowing at times when she's not home, just to keep her guessing.

———

When I get all the boards cut for the built-in, it's well past the time I usually stop for lunch and my stomach is growling louder than a table saw hitting a nail in a board. Since I have to spend the afternoon cutting and installing trim at one of my sites, I close up the shop and head toward the house. I smile as the sounds of laughter from the ladies in my grandma's origami club reach me before I even get to the door. I'm so glad she didn't have to move away from her friends.

As soon as I step through the kitchen door, a chorus of "Ian!" greets me. I smile as all the ladies seated around the table tell me how good it is to see me and how glad they are I'm here during their club.

"You all sure know how to make a guy feel like a rock star when he walks into a room."

"Honey," the white-haired Frances says, "if you ditched the flannel and donned a t-shirt and leather jacket, you'd have adoring groupies following you around wherever you went."

Brenda nods. "Especially with that perfectly mussed hair."

The hair is more a product of the air displacement from the saws and sanders than any actual styling, and I have to keep myself from reaching up and brushing some of the sawdust out of it. Instead, I wash my hands, then pull open the fridge and start pulling out lunch meat, cheese, mayo, mustard, and lettuce.

"I like the flannel," Grandma's longtime friend, Carol, says. "It's what attracted me to my dear Henry. I tell you, it was quite the trick to follow that boy around everywhere and make it seem like he was the one following me around for long enough to get him to propose." She sighs. "I would've followed him anywhere."

I chuckle as I pull a hoagie bun out of the bag and slice it open. The fact that Henry and Grandpa let me into their conversations in the work shed when I was a kid spending my summers here is a big part of why I went into carpentry. I like to imagine the two of them hanging around a band saw in heaven, still telling stories about the good old days.

"I agree about the flannel shirt," Meera says. "And with that face of yours, you could be in one of those sexy calendars filled with men in flannel." She turns back to the ladies around the table. "Don't you think he could be in a calendar, posing with that shirt?"

I smile at their conversation while I spread the mayo on my sandwich, very pointedly trying not to glance in the direction of the table but feeling every pair of eyes on me.

"Definitely," Frances says. "Especially if he posed with the sawdust still on him."

When cheers sound around the table, I'm sure my cheeks redden.

"I like to call that 'man glitter,'" Meera says, and all the ladies laugh even more.

I shoot Grandma a look, but she just shrugs, like she can't do anything about the conversation. She probably could. But she tells me every night what a "beautiful young man" I am, inside and out, and she seems to get that I think she's only saying it because she sees me through the lens of a loving grandma. Right now, she's wearing a look of triumph—one that tells me she's loving not only having her opinion validated but having it serve as proof to me that she's right.

Of course, all these ladies are wearing grandma lenses, too. I've known all of them from spending every summer here as a kid, and I've known all but one of them over the past year and a half that I've lived in Quicksand because of their bi-weekly club meetings. Brenda is the only one of Grandma's friends I haven't known as an adult—she'd moved in with her granddaughter in Phoenix to help her through cancer treatments around the same time I moved to Quicksand. This is her first club meeting back.

"You've always been such an adorable boy," Brenda says. "I'm surprised that no one has snatched you up yet."

Grandma might not shut down a conversation about my looks, but she's always quick to shut down conversations about my love life—or lack of it—and for that, I'm eternally grateful. I just need to keep stacking meats and cheeses on my sandwich while she does, then give a quick goodbye and head back out of the house, sandwich in hand.

"Do you know who would be perfect for him?" Brenda asks. "Emily Erickson. Don't you think? I was excited to see that she still lives here, and she's such an adorable girl. It's hard to believe that she's still available, too. And she could use a man as helpful and thoughtful as you. But you better act quickly, because I bet it won't take long for someone to come along and sweep her off her feet."

I can tell by the way Brenda's voice changes for that last sentence that she's directing it at me instead of the group, so I glance at the ladies as I put the top bun on my hoagie. Frances's, Carol's, and Meera's eyes are all fixed on their scattered colored paper and the intricate pieces they're folding, but Brenda's are on me. I really don't need the reminder that even though I'd been in love with Cara, I hadn't been a great catch for her in the end. I gather up the meats, cheese, and condiments and start putting them back in the fridge as quickly as possible, the familiar guilt already eating away at me.

Brenda continues on. "Have you met Lauren Pearson? She's Linda's granddaughter, and she's delightful. Oh, and speaking of granddaughters, I have one moving to Quicksand in just over a month! If you've had trouble meeting eligible women since you've been back, I'm sure that between the five of us, we could set you up with quite a few just like that." Brenda snaps her fingers.

I put my sandwich on a paper towel and quickly clean up the mess of crumbs I've made. Then I wrap the paper towel around the sandwich and hold it in one hand so I can make a quick escape. I stop by the table, though, and wrap my hand around Brenda's papery one, giving it a squeeze. "Thank you, truly, for thinking so highly of me and being willing to set me up on dates with people you respect. But I'm going to have to decline."

"Oh! Are you not single? I thought you were single." I almost pull my hand away, but she grabs hold of my forearm and turns to the other ladies around the table. "Is he not single?"

"I am," I say, then set my sandwich on the table and pat the woman's hand that still grips my arm. "It's not that. But thank you for being willing to set me up."

Brenda lets go of my arm and turns back to the table, so I grab my sandwich.

"Why would he not want to date if he's single?"

Grandma opens her mouth to answer. But before she can say anything, Meera says, "Because he got his heart ripped out 'bout a month ago. Their wedding was supposed to be a couple weekends ago, and he's still a bit broken."

I freeze where I stand.

"What?" Meera says. "It's the truth, right?"

"It's—" Grandma turns her gaze from Meera to me, her eyes clearly asking for forgiveness.

She's my grandma. I know she tells her friends everything—I wouldn't be upset with her in a million years just because Meera stated my reason in such a succinct, yet blunt, fashion. She tends to say everything with facts and force.

"Thank you for explaining for me, Meera. Now if you'll excuse me, ladies, I need to get back to work."

As I'm opening the kitchen door and escaping outside, I hear Carol say, "Don't you just love how polite he is? If anyone deserves love, it's that boy. If I had a grandson like him, I wouldn't be in the predicament I'm in now with my house."

I shake my head as I bite into my sandwich and walk toward my truck. Every once in a while, I wish I could put on a pair of grandma lenses and look at myself in the mirror to see the perfection they see.

CHAPTER 3

Addison

I PULL into a parking space at the Oregon Trail Drugstore, turn off the ignition, and slump back in my seat. Rain has been drizzling on and off all day, and the lack of sunshine for days on end is getting to me. I wonder what Matthew is doing back in Amarillo and grab my phone to pull him up on social media.

Then I stop myself. This isn't what I want—he's in my head only because of habit.

What I really want to do right now is curl up on the couch with a mug of hot chocolate and an episode of *Organize My Space*. Or even better, haul my tired bones up the stairs, pretend I don't know it's barely six p.m., collapse into bed, and sleep until morning. And not just tomorrow morning—Thursday of next week sounds nice. With the dark clouds overhead, I could probably convince myself it's night.

But as nice as that plan sounds, I have another life goal,

and that's to not stink. Since I used the last of my deodorant this morning, a drugstore visit it is. I sit up straight, put my shoulders back, pull down the visor, and slide the cover so I can see the mirror. My hair and makeup look as bedraggled as I feel, so I remove my ponytail band, run my fingers through my curls, pull my hair back into a ponytail, and put the band back on. It doesn't help much, but it's something.

I run my hands over my face, hoping to make it feel more awake, and I smile the biggest, happiest smile I can make and hold it until I feel it.

Then I force myself to say, out loud, good things that have happened to me in the past week. My rules are that the list can only contain good things, no buts allowed, and can't include anything I should've done but haven't.

"I went from having zero roommates to having three," I say. "*Me.* The girl who knew no one found three people who wanted to move into the inn with me. Girl, you are so phenomenally impressive that you even impress yourself."

And, amazingly enough, all four of us have really clicked. I hadn't had the first idea how to even go about finding roommates. Then, I happened to see a flier on the bulletin board at Gateway Groceries about a creative women entrepreneurs seminar that was taking place in two days. Since I was new at not only living in this city, living away from my sister, being single, and owning the inn but also running my own business for the first time ever, I decided to go.

And then imposter syndrome hit hard and I decided not to go.

Then, the morning of the seminar, I must've had an extra

dose of confidence because I changed my mind again and went. For one part, they put us in brainstorming groups, and my group had only women with home-based businesses. Of the eight other women, three were not only single but talked about the struggles of running a business while living in cramped quarters. I told them about the inn and *bam*! I had the three roommates I needed to cover the costs of the inn.

And to think that I almost didn't go.

Okay, that happened a few weeks ago, so I can't claim it in this week's wins, but I still give myself a literal pat on the back again for that one.

Then I chuckle at myself and then continue. "You are going to have your third weekly roommate dinner tonight, and it isn't your turn to cook." Hallelujah for that one. With as busy as my last week has been, if I had been in charge of the meal tonight, the four of us probably would've had to eat peanut butter and jelly sandwiches.

"You finished your first client home organization jobs of your brand-spankin' new business and survived." Even though one of them wanted four rooms organized, including their jewelry-making supplies. Organizing the thousands of beads ranks right up there with finding roommates.

Surviving the first few weeks felt huge. I had no idea how exhausting running my own business would be when I first decided it was my plan.

"Okay, one more." I drum my fingers on the steering wheel, thinking, and then a big smile spreads across my face. "And you successfully managed to avoid Ian Kendrick for a full four weeks." I made a fool of myself the last time I saw him when I was thirteen, and twice the very first day I saw him at twenty-six. The amount of potential embarrassment I've saved myself by avoiding him over twenty-eight days is probably astronomical.

"Nice work," I say out loud, and I feel it. Between smiling at myself and saying out loud awesome things that have happened, it's the "Give me energy, quick!" trick that works for me every single time.

I even manage to have a spring in my step as I swing my purse over my shoulder and race into the drugstore, and it's only partially because the drizzle has turned to actual rain and probably made my curls even crazier. But I find my favorite brand of deodorant, which I wasn't sure they'd have in Quicksand at all, and I toss it into my basket. Life is good.

I don't really need to buy anything else, but those bins at the back of the store are calling my name. Maybe I'll find something fun I can give to each of my new roommates.

There are other people in the store, browsing, and I manage to not pay attention to any of them. But somehow, even though I barely spot a fellow shopper at the edge of my periphery, my eyes still go to the head I can see over the top of an aisle on the far side of the store. The guy's back is to me, and as I look at the thick, dark hair with the perfect amount of wave that makes me want to run my fingers through it, I whisper, "Please don't be Ian. Please don't be Ian."

And then the man must find what he was looking for on that aisle because he turns and starts walking toward the back of the store. It's definitely Ian. And from what I can tell, the big bins at the back aisle of the store have drawn his attention, too. I glance around frantically, looking for an escape route. None of the aisles are high enough to hide me. If I dart down one, crouch to look at something, and he miraculously doesn't happen to walk down that same aisle to go to the registers, he'll still see me from the registers.

So I do the only thing I can—I crouch where I stand, which puts one of the giant bins between Ian and me. Hopefully, he didn't see me before my disappearing act. Now, all I have to do is wait for him to finish looking at whatever has drawn his attention, cross my fingers, toes, and anything else crossable, and hope he doesn't decide to wander to the bin of fuzzy socks I'm hiding behind.

I glance down the aisle I'm completely exposed to and see the teen behind the register at the other end of the store watching me with an eyebrow raised. I give him a pained smile that probably looks more like a grimace. Holding my breath so I can hear better, I strain my ears to catch any footsteps nearing over the sound of Kelly Clarkson's *Catch My Breath* coming from the speakers. Ironic.

No footsteps. Only the sound of nothing holding Kelly back. I wish something would hold Ian back.

I spent the summers here when I was ten, eleven, twelve, and thirteen. Ian didn't spend the full summer visiting his grandparents like I did, but he was here all of July. Four full months together over four years, spending a good chunk of our days playing together. It gave me plenty of opportunities to embarrass myself around him. And every time I wanted to run and hide under a rock, he would just keep putting himself right in front of me until I had to look at him, and within moments, we'd both be laughing.

I cross my fingers with more force. If he's seen me, he

isn't the kind of guy who would quietly exit the store, leaving me with dignity. And let's be honest: my dignity is in short supply at the moment. Running off to hide from embarrassment is one thing when you're ten. It's something else entirely when you're a grown woman.

Why does he have to be so good-looking now? As ridiculous as it is, I know that if he was completely unattractive, I wouldn't be hiding right now.

Hiding is stupid. I don't get embarrassed this easily normally, and I pretty much never deal with embarrassment by hiding. It's like my childhood self took over the moment I saw Ian walking toward my aisle. We're neighbors, after all. It's not like I can just avoid him forever. The awkwardness between us will eventually go away. Maybe I should just stand up with my keys in my hand, like I dropped them and was picking them up, and then face him like the adult that I am.

Or maybe I could've done that when I first crouched here, but it doesn't exactly take a full two minutes to pick up keys. Nope. At some point, I'd committed to this winner of a plan.

Was that a noise? A footstep? I hold my breath again and strain my ears. Nothing but Kelly Clarkson.

Two loud crashes sound, followed immediately by hundreds of smaller pinging crashes. The shock of it makes me shoot up from my hiding spot, whipping toward the source of the noise in alarm.

Ian is standing only a handful of feet away, next to an endcap of five shelves of Secret deodorant. The top two shelves are now lying precariously on the third shelf, and the floor around him is a sea of baby blue deodorant, a few of them still skittering to their final resting spots.

Ian meets my eyes, looks down at the sticks of deodorant covering the floor, and then glances at the employees and other customers all being pulled toward the train wreck at his feet. Then he looks at the shelves, like they've somehow betrayed him, and says, "So much for leaning here, looking all nonchalant, waiting for you to finally stand up."

He meets my eyes again, and there's something about the shocked and sheepish expression on his face that is so adorable I actually burst out with an uncontrolled laugh. Then I quickly try to stifle it. If our roles were reversed and I was in the middle of a sea of *Va Va Vanilla*-scented Secret, I wouldn't want to be laughed at. But oh, how sweet it is to finally have the roles reversed. And inexplicably, it makes it feel like I'm on even footing with Ian again.

Ian chuckles. Then he puts his fists on his hips like he's looking down at a puppy who just tore his favorite novel to shreds and says, "You're not living up to your name. Thanks a bunch, Secret."

Then he looks at me, those blue eyes sparkling. For a moment, he glances toward the registers and his confidence seems to falter, which is so unlike the Ian I remember. Then he meets my eyes again. "It's great to see you again, Addi. What do you say we get together for coffee sometime and reminisce?"

Back when we were kids, he always called me Addi. Never Addison. Hearing him say the name I've only ever been called by him instantly takes me back to our childhood and the rush of feelings of independence, excitement, and adventure. Reminiscing with the only person who lived it with me actually sounds quite nice.

It's not a date.

It's just two long-ago friends chatting about the past. That, I can do.

CHAPTER 4

Addison

I RACE from my car to the inn, holding my bag over my head to block some of the rain, then shake it off after I get under the cover of the wraparound porch and go inside. From the giant lobby where guests used to check in—a space I haven't figured out what to do with yet—I hear voices coming from the right. So I head into the kitchen and dining area where my aunt used to serve breakfast to the guests.

All three of my roommates—Bex, Peyton, and Timini—are gathered around the island, snacking on veggies and hummus.

"Addison," Peyton says, her blond ponytail bouncing as she hurries to meet me halfway to hug me. "I'm so glad you made it!"

"But you're late," Bex says with a hand on her hip, somehow looking both relaxed and fierce. Fierce, but not angry. More like she's just stating a fact.

Timini swishes her hand like she's brushing away my

lateness. "Fifteen minutes isn't even late enough to be called 'late.'" Then she brushes off an errant piece of thread from her shirt.

"I'm sorry," I say as we all sit down at the main table and Peyton goes to the oven to pull out dinner. "I got distracted by fuzzy socks at the drugstore, and then I got waylaid trying to hide from Ian."

"Listen up, Adds," Bex says, putting both hands on the table like she's about to push herself out of her seat but doesn't. Instead, it just makes her look intense. It's amazing how intimidating she can appear for as slight as her figure is. "That man is way too fine to hide from. Who cares if you embarrassed yourself in front of him once or twice?"

"I didn't only embarrass myself at the grocery store and with the movers a month ago. The summer I was here at age thirteen, I experienced my first crush ever—and it was on Ian."

"See?" Timini says, turning to Bex and Peyton. "I told you there was crushing going on."

I shake my head and just continue my story so they'll get it. "We spent a lot of time at Quicksand River that summer—and I found a great rock on the shore. It was five or six inches wide and very flat, so I painted a picture on it of the two of us holding hands and jumping into the river. I daydreamed for hours about how I was going to give it to him and how he was going to keep it by his pillow every night and think about me even after we both went back home.

"And, okay, I may have thought about it a bit too much, because when it came time to say goodbye, nerves got the best of me, and I just said, 'Here!' and shoved it into his hands. Then, instead of waiting for him to be touched by my thoughtful gift and reach for my hand and tell me how he could never forget me and that he would always treasure it, just like I had planned, I panicked and kissed him."

Bex hoots. "And what did he do?"

I shrug. "I don't know. It was a quick kiss—our lips barely had time to touch. I saw the shocked look on his face for about half a second, then I turned and ran. I hopped into my aunt's car, we drove to the airport, and I didn't see him again until four weeks ago at the grocery store. And that,"—I say, spreading my arms like I'm presenting an artifact for all to see—"was the beginning of the awkward phase of our relationship. Thirteen years later, it's still going strong."

"You know," Bex says as she leans forward and grabs from the basket a roll that looks freshly baked, "if you see him enough, it'll dilute your percentage of embarrassing moments with him."

"I mean, you'd *hope* it would," Timini says, a teasing gleam in her eye. "Unless your percentage is unnaturally high to begin with."

"No one's is *that* high," Peyton says as she nests a pan of Mushroom Florentine pasta between the rolls and a dish of asparagus.

"Or," I say, dragging out the word, "I could see him, hide behind a bin of fuzzy socks like I'm five, and in his attempt to catch me in the embarrassing moment, he could accidentally send crashing to the ground and spilling across the back of The Oregon Trail Drugstore hundreds of sticks of deodorant. And I pop up out of hiding just in time to see him standing sheepishly in a sea of Secret blue."

The laughter that erupts over the incident makes my heart do a happy dance all over again.

Bex shakes her head. "That is one effective way of lowering the percentage, girl. So are you going to stop hiding from him?"

I nod as I dish myself up some pasta. "Yeah. I am now officially fine with us being neighbors who were friends once upon a time."

"Nothing more?" Peyton asks, a look on her face like she's a kid asking for a cookie but knowing the answer is going to be no.

"Nothing more. We made a pact not to fall in love that night we decided to be roommates, remember?"

"I remember we all came here after the seminar to check the place out," Timini says.

Peyton nods. "I remember eating way too much caramel popcorn."

"Way too much," Bex says. "And I remember Timini's story about how her boyfriend sent her a breakup text saying, *It's not you, it's me. Well, me and my new girlfriend.*"

Timini chuckles. "Which I thought was pretty bad until Peyton told the story about how her ex 'mis-scheduled' a social media post that announced their breakup before he actually broke up with her."

I nod. "We all told our stories, and then we all made a pact..."

Peyton freezes in the middle of dishing up her pasta.

"Only because we were all coming off bad breakups. But oh my lands, we aren't actually sticking to that pact, are we?"

"I am," Timini says as she grabs the dish of asparagus. "But Bex isn't."

"The pact is to not 'fall in love,'" Bex says. "We said nothing about dating. I'm as dedicated to the pact now as I was then. I can date all I want—I just don't plan to fall in love."

I stab a bite of the pasta dish, getting pasta, mushroom, and spinach all together in one bite, and put it in my mouth. It's so creamy without being heavy, the flavors all perfectly combining. "Oh my, Peyton. No wonder you're so successful at your business!"

"Truth," Bex says. "I would hire you to be my personal chef any day, Pey."

Peyton looks both annoyed at the nickname Bex has been calling her since the day she moved in and pleased at the compliments. "How about your business, Addison? You've been pretty busy this past week!"

I swallow the bite I've been relishing. "I am already booked out for the next few weeks! I tell you, my sister is a genius at websites and branding and marketing."

It's such a relief. I've never really pictured myself running my own business, and I couldn't understand why people would turn down a steady paycheck from a good employer. Starting this business took almost as big of a leap of faith as moving across the country by myself did. I still can't believe Chloe managed to talk me into chasing a dream so big and uncertain, especially when she isn't even in the country to help me run it.

"Speaking of branding," Timini says, pointing her fork at each of us, "who decided to brand themselves the Post-it Queen?"

I chuckle. I've run into more than a few Post-it notes in the past five days.

Bex points her fork back at Timini, a bite of Florentine already on it. "We only have these dinners once a week. Sticky notes are a good way to communicate issues in between. Like letting someone know it's annoying when people leave stacks of fabric and sewing machines on the tables in here."

"We only use this big one," Timini says. "The other six? They can be used to run our businesses."

I should probably weigh in on the conversation since they're working out things that pertain to all of us, but I hear the faint sound of the text tone I set for only one person—my ex. I wish I'd left my phone on the check-in counter in the lobby with my purse and bag from the drugstore. But since it's right here in my pocket and I know the text came in, I can't *not* read it. It's the first time he's texted since we broke up six weeks ago.

I pull the phone from my pocket and stare at it, unable to process the words.

"Addison!" Peyton and Bex both shout my name at the same time and when I look up, I realize they must've said it several times. I don't know what look is on my face right now, and I don't know how to explain my zoning out other than just telling the truth.

"My ex, Matthew, just texted."

"Oh, no," Bex says, shaking her head.

Timini leans forward. "Does he text often?"

"What did he say?" Peyton asks.

I shake my head. "He doesn't. Not since we broke up." I look back at the text, my thumbs hovering over the keyboard. "He said he heard that I moved here, and he's asking how I like it. How should I respond?"

All three women shout that I shouldn't, and just as I look back up, a question on my face, Bex leans forward and yanks the phone from my hands.

"Seriously, don't do it," Peyton says. "It's a trap."

I look at where Bex set my phone on the table, screen side down, and then at each woman's face, confused. "How is saying something like 'I'm doing great. Thank you for asking' a trap?"

"Because, honey," Bex says, "then you'll start thinking about him again."

Peyton nods. "And wondering how he's doing."

"Before you know it," Timini says, throwing her arms up in the air, "you're wondering if you made a mistake and if you should try to work things out."

"I'm not going to—"

"Do you know what she needs?" Bex asks. "A rebound guy."

"Definitely," Timini says, then turns to me. "Our neighbor would be perfect for it. You're clearly attracted to him."

"No." I can't deny that I'm attracted to Ian. He is sweet and fun and so totally, absolutely *not* what I need right now. Even if the thought of dating him causes a happy fluttering in my stomach and spontaneous daydreams of what it would be like to be wrapped in his arms.

Yeah. Rebound dating him is the worst idea ever.

"Did you know that rebound relationships are actually healthy?" Peyton says.

I raise an eyebrow. "I'm pretty sure they're the opposite of 'healthy.'"

"No, they are!" Peyton ticks off items on her fingers as she says them. "They help you to move on and recover faster, they improve self-esteem and well-being, and they combat loneliness."

Bex puts her hand on my phone. "And they prevent unhealthy reunions with exes."

"Plus," Timini says, "they help you figure out what kind of guy complements you. Super helpful."

I stab a mushroom with my fork. "You all forgot to mention that rebound dating can keep you from properly dealing with the breakup. That's why rebound relationships rarely work out." And Matthew still crosses my mind way too much for me to believe I'm ready for a new relationship.

All three women open their mouths like they're about to say something to counter it, so I head them off with a hand like a stop sign held by a very insistent crossing guard. "Rebound relationships tend to be short. My interactions with Ian have been awkward and embarrassing enough—do you really think it's a good idea to get into a short relationship with a guy who is our next-door neighbor, and who, after our breakup, I'll still have to see practically every day?"

The thought of how awful it'd be to have a quick relationship with Ian and then to bump into him everywhere makes the tingling at the back of my neck and the tightening in my chest even stronger than when I kissed his cheek and ran off after putting the painted stone in his hand as a kid. And thoughts of dating Ian are just as exciting now as they were when I was thirteen. But it's not any more possible now than it was back then. Sure, I'm older now, but dating takes a desire to date from both people.

"I agree," Peyton says. "It definitely shouldn't be our neighbor. How about some random guy?"

I cock my head, trying to figure out why Peyton seemed like she was trying to hide something when she said that. "What aren't you saying?"

She lifts a shoulder in a shrug and keeps her eyes on her fork that's moving around mushrooms on her plate as she says, "I just think you should date anyone other than Ian."

"Why?" Timini asks. "We already know she's attracted to him."

Peyton sets her fork down and lets out a huff of a breath. "Okay. I'll say this and then nothing more because I don't even know enough to tell anything more. At the restaurant where I used to work, one of my coworkers was roommates with this girl Cara, and Cara dated Ian. They were pretty serious. I think they might have even gotten engaged.

"I saw my friend at the gym a couple of weeks ago. We were chatting and just catching up, and I asked how her roommate was doing. She said they just broke up. Anyway, it sounds like he took the breakup pretty much a thousand times harder than you are taking your breakup with Matthew, and I'm pretty sure that two people both having rebound relationships with each other isn't the best idea ever. Especially when one of them probably isn't even close to being ready."

"Oh," I say.

That explains why he seemed skittish earlier. I already don't think rebound dating is a good idea for me at all. And now I definitely don't think it sounds like a good idea for Ian. Add in the fact that being neighbors would make everything worse, and it's obvious that dating or any form of crushing on, flirting with, daydreaming about, or falling in love with is the worst idea ever.

"Well," I say, "I guess that settles it. Let's make this official: my entire goal while living in Quicksand is to *not* fall for the guy next door."

CHAPTER 5
Ian

THE DEAFENING SOUND of my portable air tank shuts off, and I use my finish nailer to put the last couple of nails into this part of the built-in. I run my hand along the section, feeling to make sure it's as smooth as it looks.

Someone whistles behind me, and I turn to see my friend and most frequent general contractor I work with, Garrett, walking into the room. "She's a beaut!"

I brush a bit of sawdust off a shelf. "Wait until you see how pretty it'll be when I finish."

Garrett comes closer to get a better look at it. "I feel bad that it's always me and not you who gets to hear homeowners praise your craftsmanship."

"Well, you do have to take all the blame for anything that goes wrong, so it seems fair."

Garrett nods. "It's true. And every time you're available to do the woodwork in a house I'm building, I figure it's the universe's way of trying to counter the complaints. I owe you, buddy. Oh, hey, guess what? Ellie just finished reading her first book by herself last night. We made a big deal about it and asked what she wanted to do to celebrate, and she said she wanted to get a pedicure at a real salon. So, of course, Emmie wants to as well, and because Ellie is Ellie, she said having her little sister there would make it more special."

"Isn't Emmie three?"

Garrett chuckles. "Yeah, so she'll probably sit on the chair for a full sixty seconds before getting down. I hope the person painting her toenails is fast. Anyway, so Paige is taking them, which leaves me free tonight. I was thinking of getting the guys together to go axe-throwing. Are you in?"

I shake my head as I root around in my bag for my putty knife and the wood filler. "I'd love to, but no can do. I've got Junior Woodworkers tonight."

"Oh, that's right. Instead of hanging out with a bunch of adult men destroying a block of wood, you'll be hanging out with a bunch of seven- to nine-year-olds destroying a block of wood."

I laugh out loud. "We've definitely destroyed some wood along the way. You'd be impressed at how good they're getting, though."

"You know, one of these days you might want to get a junior woodworker of your own."

I'm surprised it's not Cara who comes to mind immediately, as usual—it's Addi. But maybe I shouldn't be surprised. Addi is taking up more and more of my headspace all the time, and I really need to stop thinking about her. I can't face that kind of pain again anytime soon, if ever.

The damage that Cara's words inflicted when she broke off our wedding isn't the kind of thing that just goes away. It made me question everything about myself. "It's not in the cards for me, and you know it."

Garrett holds up his hands. "All I'm saying is you've got, what, four single women living in the inn next to you now? And regardless of what Cara said or what you tell yourself, you're a good man, Ian."

"I'm not interested." It's mostly the truth. I'm not interested in going through what I had with Cara ever again, and the best way to do that is to stay away from all relationships. With my elbows resting on my crouched knees, a putty knife in one hand, I let out a breath. "It looks like my wood filler isn't here. I'll have to run into town to get some." I stand up and toss the putty knife back into my bag.

"You mean this wood filler?" Garrett nudges the jar of it with his foot.

I stare down at the container. How did that get there? And why didn't I see it? But more importantly, why does it disappoint me to realize it's here?

I shake my head as it dawns on me that I was hoping to see Addi when I was in town. Like she would just appear nearby when I thought of her, like a well-timed ad on social media just when I thought of an item. I obviously need to step up my not-thinking-about-her efforts.

————

Many of the kids in Junior Woodworkers are also in Cub Scouts. Since they have their pinewood derby coming up, we spend the hour in my shop working on their cars instead of building stools, like we've been doing. Normally, I choose projects where I can teach them how to build furniture correctly and use tools properly and safely—all things my grandpa taught me—but it's fun to see their more creative sides come out in their car designs.

When we finish and the last kid is picked up by their parents, I blow most of the sawdust off myself with the air hose, then close up the shop and head into the house through the kitchen door. Grandma loves to cook, and although she doesn't cook every night, she usually does on Junior Woodworker days, knowing I'll be coming in late. And sure enough, she's got beef stew in the crock pot, and it smells great. Usually, she's in the room when I come in. I kick off my boots and head down the hall at the back of the kitchen toward the family room.

As I near, I hear voices and move closer to say hi, but I pause when I hear Addi's voice. I'm a little surprised she's in the house, considering how much she's been avoiding me. And having her here isn't exactly the best way to move forward with my not-thinking-about-her plan.

I take a few steps closer, trying to hear what they're talking about so I can guess if this will be quick or not. If it's going to be quick, maybe I'll slip back outside and clean my shop for a bit.

As I near, I can start to make out Grandma's words. "...told me how easy it was to move your things into the inn because of how organized you are. I want to be like that. And, as you can tell from all of this, I've got a long way to go."

"How long have you lived here?"

"Fifty-four years. Since I was eight months pregnant with Ian's dad. I thought I'd have to move when my dear Sheldon passed just over a year ago because this place is too much for me to care for on my own. But Ian is so sweet. He barely hesitated before packing up his stuff in Salem, buying this house, and moving in so I could stay. He's such a good boy.

"Anyway, a year ago, I started to go through everything, and all it taught me was that it's too big a job to handle on my own. So when Ian told me that you help people get organized for a living and I looked you up online..."

Their voices fade as I walk back toward the kitchen. It's sweet that Grandma is saying good things about me. It's not so sweet that I'm standing here eavesdropping. I can't tell how long they'll be—Grandma might be asking for advice, and that could take a while. I should probably head back outside to my shop.

But then I hear Grandma more clearly, so she must be close to the family room doorway. "But this isn't all of it—I need to show you my office and bedroom."

Oh no. My bedroom door is open, and I know for a fact that I didn't make my bed this morning. I'm not sure, but I might possibly have a dirty shirt or two on the floor. My room isn't too messy, but it's not something someone like Addi would call "organized."

When we were kids, it wasn't weird at all to have her in my room. When we visited here each summer, my brothers and I shared the room I live in now, and it's where we kept the Legos. But now that Addi and I are adults and don't know each other as well as we once did, it feels strange having her in my house. And it would feel even stranger to have her seeing my things. And if Grandma is showing Addi her office, they'll need to walk right past my room.

I can't go toward the family room and get to my bedroom hall from that direction, since that's where they are. So I race into the living room and head into the hall from the opposite way. I come at my room a little too fast and bang my arm, from shoulder down to elbow, into the doorframe, making a loud thud. But I manage to pull my door shut just before Grandma and Addi round the corner.

"Oh my goodness," Grandma says, looking around, "what was that bang?"

I shrug and then wrap an arm around Grandma's shoulders, giving her a hug. Then I turn to Addi. "Hello, Addi. I wasn't expecting to see you here. How are you?"

Once upon a time, I was good at talking to girls. Somewhere along the way, probably after ending things with Cara, I must've forgotten how. Seriously, "I wasn't expecting to see you here" is the best I can do?

"Oh, hi, Ian. Your grandma didn't think you'd be back so soon."

I glance at Grandma and catch the hint of a smile before she hides it. I always come in at the same time on Junior Woodworkers days.

"Addison is every bit as amazing as you said she was."

Addi ducks her head, but I think I catch a bit of a blush before she does. To tell the truth, I'm feeling a little warm around the ears, too. I told Grandma that Addi was good at what she does—I didn't think she'd make it sound like I talk about Addi nonstop. That's only partly true.

"I asked her to come over to see what she could do for me and all the stuff I've collected over the years. That way, when I die, all that work won't be left to family. Now don't worry, I don't plan on dying anytime soon. But I tell you what—this girl here is in high demand. Probably because everyone figured out how good she is. I thought I wouldn't have a chance swaying her to help me, but she says she's going to stop by in the evenings and on weekends, just to help an old woman out."

Then Grandma winks at me, and she's not exactly subtle about it.

"Your grandma was pretty hard to say no to when we were kids," Addi says, then shrugs, "and she's just as hard to say no to now. And of course, I'm happy to help a neighbor out."

Addi's golden brown hair is pulled into a loose bun, and with the mass of curls she has, it's beautiful. I especially like how a few curls have escaped and fallen next to her slender neck. A lot about her has changed over the years. Not those mischievous green eyes I remember so well from our childhood, though.

Grandma beams at her. "Isn't she the best?"

I realize I'm gazing at her. I clear my throat and say, "So, you're going to be here a lot after work, huh?"

She eyes me, and I can't read the expression on her face. Is she happy about that? Sad? Wary? I'm not even sure what expression is on my own face. Part of me is smiling just thinking about how she won't be able to easily duck out or hide when I'm around. The much bigger part of me is terrified to have someone I'm attracted to—and thinking about way too much to be healthy—be so close.

"Just two or three times a week."

Okay, then. Two or three times a week, I need to silence the part of me that wants to see her and give the terrified part free rein to find reasons why I suddenly have to be away from home.

CHAPTER 6

Addison

I MISS CHLOE. I'm used to talking to my sister daily and texting dozens of times a day. When I walk through the door of the inn and drop my purse and keys on the reservation counter, I glance at the clock on my phone. It's been an incredibly long day organizing a shoe and jewelry hoarder's bedroom all the way over in Lake Oswego, and I'm beat. But I do the math, and it's after 3 a.m. in Paris, so a phone call is out of the question.

Instead, I send a text. *Call me when you're free to talk business strategy?* My business started out with a bang, mostly because of Chloe's genius, but my openings further out aren't being filled as quickly as I'd like, and it's making me a bit nervous. I hesitate a moment, phone still in hand, then send a second text. *And maybe chat a bit about my neighbor.*

There. I sent it. Chloe will grill me about it, but she'll also let me talk through things without too much judgment. It's not that I *want* to be thinking about Ian. But my subconscious doesn't seem to get that memo, so my mind keeps wandering to him without my permission.

I glance at the stairs, thinking about how nice it would be to go up, flop on my bed, and stream a TV show until I get some energy back. But my body is already turning toward the kitchen, and I'm mentally going through what food is in the fridge and how much effort it would take to put something in my grumbling stomach.

My stomach growls even louder just thinking about my options. Food it is. Maybe that will replenish my energy. I head into the kitchen and find Bex at her laptop, with a smile on her face that says she's either editing one of her YouTube videos or replying to comments from her fans. She glances at me but keeps working, so I go to the fridge. Yes! Peyton made enchiladas and put an *Anyone can eat* sticky note on the top.

I'm just putting a plate with two enchiladas on it into the microwave when Bex must've finished what she was working on, shuts her laptop, and turns toward me. "So... I saw our neighbor today."

"Yeah?" I try to make the word sound uninterested. I might even succeed.

"He'd just walked out of his shed and was brushing sawdust off those muscled arms and chest."

I turn around to face her. "Bex."

"I'm just saying that maybe you should reconsider dating him."

"You're still pushing that? Even after hearing that he's just coming off a hard breakup?"

"You moved in, what, five weeks ago? And his relationship ended sometime before then. Maybe he needs a little rebound dating, too."

As the microwave does its thing, I lean against the counter behind me, arms folded, shaking my head at Bex's tenacity. "Even if you took away all the problems of rebound dating for each of us, it's not like dating someone is all my choice. It takes two people."

"And?"

"And," I let out a frustrated breath, dropping my arms, "I've never had guys lining up at my door. I've had plenty of crushes before—guys I really would've liked to have dated —but that didn't mean they felt the same way." It was probably a big chunk of the reason why I stayed with Matthew for as long as I did. The whole time, a part of me knew that if we broke up, I might go a very long time before dating someone new, whether I liked it or not.

Bex looks at me like she's confused or like I'm crazy. Bex has probably never experienced being interested in dating someone and not having him feel the same. "But you're gorgeous."

I shake my head and then run my fingers through my long curls, looking at them as I do. "I know the hair attracts men. Enough that we start chatting and texting and getting to know each other. And then, before we ever get to 'We should go out sometime,' they're coming to me for dating advice. I'm the friend, never the girlfriend. Even if I did want to date Ian—*which I don't.* I just got out of a two-year relationship, after all—it doesn't mean the choice is all up to me. And I can tell that Ian's just not interested in going out with me."

Before Bex can respond, we both stand up straighter and cock our heads toward the sound of a lawnmower starting.

"Is that in our yard?"

Instead of answering, I race back out into the front lobby and then into the gathering room, Bex on my heels as we run by the couches and chairs in the large area. At first, we can't see any sign of the lawnmower in the backyard. Then, a few seconds later, it appears from behind some shrubs that hide the maintenance shed, being pushed by none other than our neighbor, Ian.

"Ian's been the one mowing?" Bex asks.

Maybe I should've guessed—it was Ian and his brothers who took care of the yard as kids when they were here for the summers. But who would've guessed he'd still be doing it now?

"You should go talk to him. Your car is parked on the side by his house, so he has to know you're home. It'd be rude if you saw it was him and didn't thank him. I mean, *I* could thank him, but I don't own the building, so it wouldn't carry as much weight coming from me. I think it has to be you."

I take a deep breath. "You're right. It's the neighborly thing to do."

I stop by the downstairs bathroom to make sure my hair isn't too crazy, and then I head out the back door. Ian has just turned to mow the next strip, so his back is to me as he mows the length of the yard. I wait. I tell myself it's not so I can watch him—it would simply be rude to walk behind him when he can't hear me coming.

Seeing him mow now is nothing like seeing him push the

mower when he was eleven or even fourteen. The last thirteen years have definitely treated him well. Especially in his shoulders and the top of his back, where his muscles are showing very clearly through the fabric of his t-shirt. He doesn't know I'm watching, though, so I start feeling like a stalker and walk out to meet him instead.

I'm still a good fifteen feet away when he reaches the end of the yard and turns the mower so he's facing me again. He shuts it off as soon as he sees me. He glances at the part of the lawn he's already cut, then scratches the back of his neck. "Looks like I'm busted."

I laugh as I take the last few steps toward him. "Have you been mowing all this time? Why didn't you tell me?"

"I have. I've never stayed next door and not taken care of this yard, so it feels wrong not to. As far as why I haven't told you…" He lifts one of those strong shoulders in a shrug. "Everyone loves a mystery, right? I was just giving you one."

That makes me smile. Of course, he did. "Did my aunt line up payment with you before she died? Do I owe you past lawn mowing fees?"

"She used to pay us when we were kids. But growing up, my brothers and I did a lot of yard care for others in Salem, and my dad's rule was that we had to mow at least one yard a week for someone who needed it and not charge them. When I moved back here more than a year ago, the inn became my one yard a week."

That is so sweet. And to still be doing it now, when he's no longer mowing lawns as a kid for money and therefore obligated to mow one for free. Maybe that's why his eyes look so kind—because he genuinely is.

I realize I'm looking into those eyes a little too deeply and shake myself out of my stupor. "I want to do something to thank you. I'm not much of a baker, but I'm pretty good at buying baked goods. Maybe I could get a pie, or cupcakes, or… ice cream! Not that ice cream is a baked good."

"How about coffee?"

He's smiling that adorable amused smile, and it suddenly makes me forget what we're talking about. "You want me to bake you coffee?" My brow crinkles. "Oh! We had plans to go get coffee and catch up. Right."

"Tomorrow after work?"

I nod. "Tomorrow it is."

As I walk back to the inn, knowing he's watching me, I'm hyper-aware of how I'm walking and suddenly can't remember how to walk normally. But it's definitely not whatever I'm doing right now. I can't even talk to him normally. What is wrong with me?

It's probably his eyes.

Yeah, it's definitely those eyes that are throwing me off. The eyes that are the same blue as the sky I painted on that rock back when I first forgot how to talk around him. All I have to do is avoid the eyes, and I'll be just fine.

———

After I grab the enchiladas I nearly forgot about from the microwave, I head up to my room and sit at my desk with my laptop. As it boots, I take a bite of the dish that makes me, once again, so grateful Peyton is a roommate. Then I open a browser and type in the search bar, *How to stay away from a rebound relationship.*

The results show links to several articles about how to tell if you're in a rebound relationship, but I have to scroll quite a bit to find one about how to keep from getting into one. Unfortunately, there isn't one titled *How to keep from falling a little more for your neighbor every time you see him.*

So I remind myself that rebound dating = bad. Bad for me, bad for Ian. Even if his eyes are kind and beautiful. Even if his jawline is pretty near perfect. Even if he looks incredible mowing the lawn or covered in sawdust as he tries to surreptitiously close his bedroom door before I can see inside. Even if he does things like buy a house so he can help his grandma, mow people's lawns to be nice, or volunteer to teach kids woodworking skills. None of that matters, because *rebound dating = bad.*

Maybe I should write it in giant letters on my arm with a marker so I can't forget.

I'm only partway through the article when I grab a notebook and start writing down things I need to remember to keep myself from being attracted to Ian. I write in all caps across the top of the page, *HOW TO NOT FALL FOR THE GUY NEXT DOOR.* Then I make my list of things from the article.

> —*If you want to date someone just to make your ex jealous, <u>you're not ready to date</u>.*
> —*If you hope your ex will call and let you know how he's doing, <u>you're not ready to date</u>.*

> *—If you think of your ex constantly, <u>you're not
    ready to date</u>.*
> *—If you struggle to delete photos of your ex, <u>you're
    not ready to date</u>.*
> *—If you have a hard time deleting your ex's phone
    number, <u>you're not ready to date</u>.*
> *—If you're still pining over your ex, <u>you're not ready
    to date</u>.*
> *—If you're still looking at your ex's social media,
    <u>you're not ready to date</u>.*
> *—If you're rushing a new relationship because of a
    sense of urgency, <u>you're not ready to date</u>.*

Then I add one more that the article doesn't mention but is important for me to remember.

> *—If your neighbor experiences any of the above, <u>then
    he's not ready to date, either</u>.*

I look over what I've written. Matthew lives seventeen hundred miles away, so it's not like he'll ever see if I date anyone else. So I'm pretty safe with that first one. I still think about Matthew too much and often wonder how he's doing, but I've been fairly good at the other things. Mostly. More than how much I'm thinking of Matthew, I should probably be concerned about how often I'm thinking of Ian.

I'm making progress on all the items, though, and that's what matters. It's a good list to keep in mind. If I ever catch myself doing any of those things, I'll know I'm not ready to move on.

Just like writing *I won't run in the halls* a hundred times when I broke the rule in fourth grade, writing *You're not ready to date* so many times, underlining it each time, has actually helped my mindset.

Actually, two of the things don't need to be on the list at all. I open my phone, go to the photos app, and delete the entire folder with pictures of Matthew and me together. Then I go into my contacts and delete his number. It feels good! Healthy. Wise. Powerful.

Grinning widely, I cross both items off my list with as much glee as my high school English Lit teacher marked up my *Hamlet* essay.

Not that I'm aiming to just cross all the items off the list. I'm in Quicksand for a fresh start, and that means figuring out what I want out of life without a boyfriend affecting the plan.

No, this isn't a list of things to accomplish so I can move on to something new. This is a list to help keep myself from falling for Ian.

CHAPTER 7

Ian

I SIT on a bench at the trailhead park, smiling as Addi pulls into the parking lot slowly. Then she looks down, probably at her phone. She looks back at the road she just turned off before she glances toward the trail and spots me. She smiles and pulls into a parking space.

I hope she's up for walking the trail. Sitting across from each other in a coffee shop where all we can do is stare into each other's eyes while we talk feels too much like a date and not like old friends catching up. I remind myself, once again, that's all this is. I stand as she opens her door and steps out of her car.

"It's a good thing you were sitting where I could see you —I thought I got the address wrong. This isn't exactly a coffee shop."

She's come straight from work and is wearing dark jeans that are fitted and make her legs look incredible. She has on a flowy pink blouse, which is a little dressy for a walk in the woods, but at least she's wearing flats. If I were spending the day organizing someone's house, I'd probably show up in a t-shirt, jeans, and athletic shoes. I assumed Addi would be dressed similarly, so I didn't anticipate that changing up the plan would be an issue.

"No, but since we've had a few rain-free days, I thought a walk along Chipper Creek Trail might be more fun than a stuffy coffee shop. Plus," I turn to grab the two cups of coffee I already picked up from Doug's Donuts and hold one out to her, "I've got coffee."

Addi looks at the cup for a long moment before taking it. "I was supposed to pay for coffee, remember?"

"But then I changed up what we're doing without warning you or giving you a chance to dress for it. Let's consider us even."

"We're even, then," she says and bumps her cup into mine. I'm loving this sunny day even more as I gaze at how it lights up Addi's face and hair. It gives both a golden glow that is breathtaking on her. And those mischievous eyes I love are looking more golden than hazel.

Okay, I've got to stop noticing every detail about her.

Addi's gaze shifts over my shoulder to the trailhead. "I haven't even thought about this place in so long. I used to love coming here as a kid."

"If you'd rather not in those shoes—"

"No, I'm good." She starts walking toward the trailhead purposely like she's afraid I'll change my mind. We've only walked on the trail for maybe a dozen feet before she says, "It still blows my mind how green everything is here."

I've lived in Oregon my entire life, so this trail is nothing new. But Addi only spent four summers here half her life-time ago, and I imagine the surroundings are a bit different than in Amarillo. I try to look at the thick forest filled with green things growing at all different heights through her eyes. It's beautiful as always, but I haven't really paid attention to exactly how green everything is until I picture how it must look to a girl who grew up in an area with wide, open spaces and rainstorms that don't occur every few days.

"In Amarillo, everything is so brown. I mean, not in town so much—people have grassy yards—but if you get out of town at all, there are so many shades of brown. There's no brown here."

I haven't ever thought about it, but she's right. Even the tree trunks are green here with all the moss that grows on them.

The trail isn't crowded, but there are people ahead of us, and a few pass by walking in the opposite direction every few minutes. Mostly, it's just the sound of our feet on the crushed gravel trail as I ask her about how work is going, and she asks me the same as we sip our coffees.

As much as I like talking to her about what's going on with us now, I'm dying to ask her about what happened thirteen years ago. As soon as the conversation moves past enough pleasantries to be polite, I say, "When you were last here, you said you'd see me the next summer, but you never came back."

Smooth, Ian. Could you be any more blunt?

"It wasn't my fault, I swear. My little sister, Chloe, never came with me to Aunt Helen's because she was into fashion marketing from pretty much the day she was born, so she always went to Fashion Designer Camp. The year I was thirteen and she was eleven, she came home from camp with a portfolio of her work." She glances over at me. "I know. Overachiever, right?"

I chuckle.

"Anyway, it made my parents decide that it was time I stopped spending my summers playing and started spending them developing skills. I went on a bunch of week-long camps every summer until I was sixteen and had a job. So, I went to," she says, ticking each item off on her fingers as she says them, "soccer camp, young explorers camp, drama camp, young novelists camp, leadership camp, space camp—you name the camp, I probably did it."

For years, I'd wondered if she never came back because my reaction to her gift and kiss was to freeze and not say a thing. I didn't realize it was still weighing on me until her explanation lifted the weight. "No Organizer's Anonymous Camp?"

I soak in the sound of her laughter as we walk onto one of the five bridges that cross the meandering stream. "No, surprisingly, based on the variety of ones I went to. And even though one probably didn't exist, I didn't have every second of my future planned out at age fourteen enough to know I even wanted that. I still don't let Chloe forget how she ruined my summers with her unnaturally young career planning."

She stops to lean over the bridge's railing and look at the water, so I do, too. After a moment, Addi says, "I miss Aunt Helen."

I nod. "I do, too. She was a phenomenal woman."

"She was, wasn't she? I'm lucky I got to spend so many summers with her. I wouldn't be who I am without her."

We are both silent for a long moment as we just watch the water pass by below us. Then Addi says, "Remember when we were kids and your grandma taught us how to make origami boats out of waxed paper, and we'd drop them off at one bridge, and then race down the trail and try to beat them to the next bridge?"

I laugh at the memory. "And the boats always won, except at the very end of summer when there wasn't as much water flowing. And then, half the time, it was because they got stuck along the way."

She turns to me. "Let's go down by the stream." Her smile lights up her face and makes me smile. It had when we were kids, too, but somewhere along the way, her smile became even more beautiful. Mesmerizing.

We walk to the end of the bridge, toss our coffee cups in the garbage can at the bridge's edge, and head down to the water. I should've known—water always draws Addi to it. It was why we spent so many of our summer days either here by Chipper Creek or in our favorite cove at Quicksand River.

I'm glad to know she didn't stop coming to spend her summers with her aunt because of me. But I'm still curious about that kiss she shocked me with. I step up next to her, and we both watch a squirrel race to the water's edge, then scurry back, then to the creek again, each time getting closer and closer to us. "So, you know that painted stone you gave me? I still have it."

Addi's attention flies right to me, a surprised look on her face. "You kept it all these years?"

"I was hoping to one day ask you about it again." Her eyes search mine, and I work up the courage—and try to come up with the wording—to ask if she kissed me because she liked me, or if it was just a friendly goodbye, but every sentence I think of sounds awful. It's not like I need to know so I can sleep better at night or anything. Well, okay, that knowledge probably would've helped me sleep better back when I was fourteen. But I hadn't thought about it for years before seeing her again in Gateway Groceries.

Maybe just letting it go again is the best thing. But I feel like I owe it to the fourteen-year-old me to just spit the question out, no matter how awful it sounds, so I don't have to wonder.

I'm just opening my mouth to ask when a dog's barking gets rapidly closer, right along with shouts from the dog's owner. Both Addi and I turn in time to see a large dog racing toward us—or, more likely, the squirrel that had been very near us—with its leash bouncing behind it as it hits rocks and tufts of weeds, its owner chasing after it. Neither of us has time to react before the dog plows into Addi, knocking her backward.

I grab her arm as she falls, and between the efforts of both of us, she manages to stay upright, even though she has to take a giant step into the stream to stop her fall. The dog takes off in the direction of the squirrel just as quickly as it came, leaving both of us breathing heavily from the adrenaline of it all.

"Are you okay?"

She nods, and I pull her toward me and out of the stream. As soon as she lifts the foot that had been deepest in the water, though, the rushing stream grabs hold of her shoe, which, as a slip-on, has only about two inches holding it to the top of her foot, and sends it downstream.

"No!" Addi shouts, lunging for it.

"I've got it," I yell, racing after the shoe. Within moments, though, it reaches the next bridge and passes beneath it. The bridge is too low to duck under, so I race around the structure that suddenly seems overly massive for the size of the stream, and then I dash alongside the water's edge. The shoe is ahead of me by a couple hundred feet. I leap over rocks and tree stumps and fallen branches as I run after it. But no matter how fast I go, it keeps getting further and further away.

Finally, I realize what a lost cause it is, and how my chasing it down the river has left Addi balancing on one foot upstream. I jog back to where I abandoned her to find her making her way back up to the trail, doing a mix of hopping and touching just the ball of her foot down on the most rock-free parts of the ground. I race to her side, and she puts an arm around my back to steady herself.

"I'm so sorry, Addi. I swear it took your shoe down-stream even faster than it took our boats." I glance at the foot that still wears a shoe. "They looked new, too."

"Today was my first time wearing them."

I cringe.

"But they've been killing my feet all day. They aren't nearly as comfortable as the website made them look."

"Your feet have been hurting all day in those shoes, and yet you still agreed to walk the trail?"

She shrugs. "It's not much different from wearing heels

on a date." Her eyes go wide, clearly shocked at what she just said. "Not that this is a date! I didn't mean that. I just meant… Friends. Catching up. This is a 'friends catching up' get-together."

"I've missed you, Addi." I'd forgotten how much being around her ratchets my happiness level up. Or how much I love the blush that frequently lights up her face.

We both look at the trail. Sure, down by the water there are rocky areas as much as there are patches of grassy weeds and dirt. But the trail itself is crushed gravel—the kind you definitely don't want to walk on barefoot.

She's right. We're just old friends catching up. This isn't a date. But still, I've been feeling an attraction to Addi pulling me the entire time. So, I know how much what I'm about to do will take me to very dangerous territory, but I offer anyway. "Well, I guess there's only one solution: I'll have to carry you back."

"What? No. That's like half a mile, Ian. You can't do that. Your arms will want to fall off if you carry me that far."

"You have that little faith in my muscles?" She checks out my muscles, and she blushes again. I have to admit, it makes me feel pretty great. "All right, then. Ready?"

She nods, and I pick her up, one arm around her back and one under her knees. She wraps an arm around my neck to hold on. With her in my arms, her arm around me, her face so close to mine, all my reminders to myself that we're nothing more than old friends fly away faster than her shoe going down the river.

Right now is the point when I should very emphatically remind myself that I never want to date again, and even if I miraculously did, it's too soon, so I should keep my distance. But that voice just as quickly fades away in the breeze. Apparently, too big a part of me wants to just let myself be in the moment.

And that's all it is. A moment. Nothing serious. Just old friends.

"Do you know what else I kept?" I'm so close to her, all I have to do is whisper.

She barely shakes her head no, like nothing more is needed while we're in such close proximity.

"Those cheesy rhymes you used to write whenever we got on each other's nerves and you wanted to lead me to where you were hiding so we could make up."

"No," she says, dragging out the word. "You didn't."

"I so did. Every last one."

Her ears turn pink, and she looks out at the woods for a moment before meeting my eyes again. "Seriously. Tell me you didn't."

"They were pretty catchy rhymes. Let me think—I might still have my favorite one from when you were ten or eleven memorized." I gaze up at the sky. It's been a long time since I thought of it, but I still have the preamble to the Constitution in my brain from memorizing it in eighth grade. So that has to mean that I have her rhyme in my head, too, because I cared a lot more about memorizing it than I did the preamble.

I clear my throat. "'You said my Lego door was dumb, which made me mad!'"

"Stop it."

"'You told me sorry, but I wasn't done being sad.'"

"Ian."

"'I am now, so go where I stuck my gum on that tree stump. Walk fifteen steps until you come to the grass clump.'"

She's laughing now.

"'Then go left and run forty big, giant paces. Turn around and you'll see where my hiding place is.'"

The pink is all across her cheeks now, and I can feel her laughing against my chest. "I cannot believe you remember that. That was the time I sat in my hiding place for thirty minutes, and you never came."

"Only because you never said in your rhyme in which direction I should walk the fifteen steps, and I chose the wrong direction because that entire field was covered in grass clumps. And then Mrs. Walters got mad at me for running twenty-two of the forty big, giant paces through her garden."

She laughs again, and the sound feels like home out here. Like birds singing in the trees.

"I took a poetry class in college. I think my professor would tell you that my skill in writing poetry hasn't improved since I was a kid."

"Suddenly, I want nothing more than to read your poetry written as an adult." No, that's wrong. There is something I want more.

A smile spreads across my face as I realize I'm much more likely to get an answer with her in my arms than while she's in the path of a dog on a mission. "But first, a question." A genuine smile crosses my face as I watch her expression. "When you left your aunt's inn to head back to the airport that last summer and you kissed me, was that a new way of saying goodbye that you were trying out, or did you kiss me because you liked me?"

Addi laughs and looks up at the sky, shaking her head. I'm not sure she's going to answer, but then she meets my eyes again. "I had a crush on you, okay? It was my first one ever, and I obviously wasn't very good at it. The painted stone was so that you'd think of me often while I was in another state."

I smile doubly—for the fourteen-year-old me and the twenty-seven-year-old me—as I look at the path ahead. "Well, I have to say that your plan worked."

CHAPTER 8
Addison

I'VE BEEN HELPING Ian's grandmother organize her origami supplies in their family room for a grand total of about eight minutes when Ian gets home from work. Based on the feigned surprise on Shirley's face at him being home and Ian's confusion at her surprise, I get the distinct impression she's playing matchmaker. Too bad she didn't have me come over early enough that I could've told her about my recent breakup and how I'm not ready for anything new yet.

And especially not with a guy who's recovering from his own breakup and happens to be my next-door neighbor.

Two weeks ago, when Ian carried me—minus one shoe— back to my car, something changed. Maybe it was from having our faces so close together that we could feel each other's breath as we talked. Or maybe it was because of how perfect it felt to be held by him. Or because I had my arm around his shoulders, holding tight.

Or the fact that he offered to carry me in the first place.

He could've just been a support, walking next to me as I hopped back to my car. Or he could've left me at the side of the river while he drove to get another shoe from my apartment. But he didn't—he *carried* me.

Maybe the change I'm sure we both felt two weeks ago was simply a product of proximity. Like when two magnets stick together when they are near each other. But it's not like we search each other out from across the room when we aren't close. We don't feel the pull unless we're near. It's nothing but proximity.

Because if it were more than proximity, it would've pulled him to me before now. During the last two weeks, he's been avoiding me as expertly as I avoided him before the big deodorant debacle in the drugstore. Several times, we've accidentally run into each other, as neighbors do. But each time, his small talk feels forced, like I'm a long-winded neighbor with a differing political opinion or endless cat stories and he's trying to get away to avoid hearing them.

Whether we acted like magnets for that half mile two weeks ago or not, it's not that way now. I tell myself it's a relief because I'm not ready for a relationship. I don't know how long ago he and his fiancée broke up, but it's obvious he isn't looking for a relationship either. I can tell because I've been at his house several times over the past few weeks, helping his grandma, and each time he's suddenly had things he needed to do that have kept him away.

He underestimates his grandma's ability to get him to help with this project, though.

I brought several storage pieces that will work together to organize all Shirley's colored paper squares and rectangles and her origami books. The biggest issue with organizing her hobby is what to do with all the unique origami creations she's made that are currently living in cardboard boxes stacked on top of each other.

"Ian?" Shirley calls out. "Can you come here for a minute?"

When Ian walks into the family room at the back of the house, she says, "Addison came up with a plan to showcase my origami pieces, and since it'll change the look of the room, I want to know what you think about it."

"Grandma, you know I'll be okay with it. This is your home, too. You can display your things however you'd like."

"And it's also your home. So zip it and listen to Addison's plan."

I hide a smile and explain to Ian that I suggested we hang each of the paper creations from the ceiling using fishing line so it wouldn't be seen. "We'll do it at all different heights just in front of this blank wall, so it'll be an art installation—a masterpiece people can spend a while looking at."

"I love it."

"Wonderful!" Shirley claps her hands. "Because we're going to need help installing it. You're free tonight, right?"

My eyes flash to Shirley as my chest tightens. I definitely didn't say anything about needing help. Ian's expression is every bit as alarmed as mine.

"What?" Shirley says to me, trying to look innocent. "We *do* need help. Getting on a ladder without someone supporting it isn't wise, and these arms aren't as supportive as they once were."

So, as Shirley lays out each of her creations along the

floor, adjusting which ones are where and changing up the heights on all of them until she likes the way they look, Ian and I sit on the floor, cutting lengths of fishing line and tying them to each piece. Actually, it doesn't feel so different from when we were kids, sitting side by side, making Lego villages. It's kind of fun.

I imagine doing this same thing with Matthew. Unplanned. And on a Thursday night. I nearly laugh out loud. If I had somehow gotten him to do a crazy project like this, there's no way I would've gotten him to sit on the floor to do it.

And there I go, accidentally thinking about my ex again. Obviously, I should squash any feelings I have toward Ian right now before my heart thinks it can get invested any more than it already is.

Except Ian is so sweet to his grandma, and he's so patient. Every time he talks to her while sitting on the floor and tying fishing line to a folded piece of paper with his big hands that somehow don't hinder his ability to work with something so delicate, it makes him that much more attractive. It makes those eyes of his even more beautiful.

Those eyes are going to be my undoing.

Seriously, Addison. Squash those feelings!

It takes a while, but we eventually get the line tied to all four dozen origami pieces and bring out the ladder to start attaching them to the ceiling. While Shirley chats about how the summers weren't the same once I stopped coming to Hidden Inn and how sad it was for Ian, especially that first summer I wasn't here, I put the ladder in place and hang the first couple. Ian dutifully holds onto the side of the ladder, just as his grandma requested, even though it feels completely unnecessary.

Each time I step onto the ladder, I'm acutely aware of how close we are to each other. So is my stomach, apparently, because it fills with butterflies. We're not holding onto each other like we did at Chipper Creek, yet I swear the butterflies are flapping even stronger—like maybe they drank caffeine instead of nectar.

The same as when we were kids, I can sense Ian's emotions just by looking at him. He's feeling something, too, like he was when he was carrying me.

When I finish hanging a cute little origami frog, Ian hands me the next one so I don't have to get off the ladder. And when I take it from him, our hands brush, and it sends a thrill across my skin. It's like Shirley picked up those magnets from opposite sides of the room and put them next to each other again.

And we've got some pretty strong magnets. I so need to get some distance from this man!

Especially because after I move the ladder to the next spot—and the next four spots after that—Ian conveniently turns to say something to his grandma every time I'm climbing the ladder at the moment when our faces would've been so close if he hadn't turned. And when he hands me the fishing line for the next one, he holds it in a way that I can grab it without touching his hand. He clearly doesn't want our magnetic selves to be so close, either.

When we've hung the colorful creations about two-thirds of the way across the long wall, I hear the faint sound of my sister's ringtone, so I quickly pull out my phone to see if it's really her.

Still looking at the phone, my eyebrows crease. "This is my sister, and it's the middle of the night where she is. Do you mind if I take this?"

"You go right ahead," Shirley says.

I answer as I'm walking through the kitchen to the back door. "Chloe! Is everything okay?"

"Everything's so good!"

I step outside and shut the door behind me. "Isn't it after two in Paris?"

"Yep. Dustin and I went to the most amazing fashion show and after-party tonight. I got to meet so many of my idols! When we got home, Dustin crashed in about four seconds flat, but I'm still too wired to sleep, so I thought I'd call."

"I love that you're getting so many opportunities to do what you love! Even if it does mean that you're not in my city. Or state. Or country."

"Yeah, that's definitely been the worst part. So how are things going with you? Have you seen Ian much since you went on that not-a-date coffee walk with him through the woods?"

I glance back toward the house, almost like I'm checking to make sure he can't hear from where he is, which is ridiculous. "I'm at his house right now, actually. Just helping his grandma."

"Interesting. Also, I still think you lost your shoe in the creek on purpose. If you'll admit it, then I'll admit it was a brilliant plan."

"It wasn't on purpose—they were really cute shoes, even. Uncomfortable as could be, but super cute. And brand new. Also, I'm not brilliant, or I wouldn't be over here at his house, reminiscing about the creek with every glance or accidental touch. Especially when I know it's going nowhere."

"No. Don't you be talking like that's the most that's ever going to happen between you two. He was your first crush, and it took fate to bring you together again. It's practically meant to happen."

"Chloe, he doesn't want it to. He's making it very clear that whatever we shared on that walk was a fluke. He's not interested, and neither am I. I'm just not ready to date again yet."

Chloe lets out a long sigh, like she doesn't really agree with me but is humoring me. "How will you know when you are ready?"

"The websites I saw said it usually takes a good three months before dating again won't be a rebound. Matthew and I broke up nine weeks ago, so I've got about a month to go. By the time I'm ready, Ian will have forgotten all about our walk in the woods."

"Okay."

"Chloe," I say cautiously, "why were you smiling when you said 'Okay'? Tell me."

My sister chuckles quietly. "I just can't wait to see if fate agrees with your timeline."

CHAPTER 9

Ian

I WALK into the bowling alley later than I'd planned and look around for the guys. I wish I'd been free on axe-throwing night—I enjoy that more than bowling. But I'm really just here to see the guys.

Garrett stands and waves, and I wave back before stopping at the counter to pay and get shoes. When I head over to the lane the guys are already at, I see Garrett's wife, Andre's girlfriend, and a woman with Isaac that I haven't seen before. When I get to the bench, Garrett sits next to me.

"Is the Williamson house still giving you troubles? I was beginning to think you wouldn't make it."

"It's been putting up a good fight, that's for sure. I didn't want to leave before I finished the trim. Was it date night tonight?"

"Sorry about that. It wasn't going to be, but Paige's mom asked if she could take our kids tonight, so I didn't want to come without her. I didn't know that Andre was bringing

Rose, and the woman with Isaac is someone he met here. I should've texted you."

"No, it's fine," I say, and it is. Because I also know that if Garrett had texted, I likely wouldn't have shown up at all. I dated Cara for long enough that I got used to constantly having a date for things. I'm still not used to being the only dateless one in a group.

Since there are seven of us, we've got both of the lanes that share the seating area, and the other two guys and their dates are already playing in their lane, which leaves Garrett, Paige, and me in ours. Paige finishes putting our names on the screen, and the three of us start bowling.

Work today was frustrating. It took a long time to get everything perfect in some really unusual and intricate areas, and it feels good to relax with the guys. They're a fun group, even if I often feel the pain of being alone. They're quick to laugh and joke around, and Addi would probably love hanging out with them.

The thought surprises me. I need to get her out of my head better than I've been doing.

On the third frame, I get a strike and high-five everyone as I walk back to the bench and sit by Paige while Garrett gets up to bowl his frame.

"So, what's new, Ian?" she asks.

"Not much. How about you?" I assume the question is basic small talk until she shifts on the bench to look at me as she talks.

"No, I meant for real, what is new? There's something about you that's... different."

My first thought is Addi. Which is stupid because it's not like I'm around her that much.

"Um, I got a haircut last week."

Paige raises an eyebrow and her lips quirk up in a smile. "Yeah. Haircut. I'm sure that's it." She gives her husband a double high-five as he walks back after getting nine pins down and waits for his ball to come back up through the chute.

The waiting gets ridiculously long, though, so Garrett's eyebrows come together, and he looks toward the shoe rental counter. "I think my ball got stuck. I'm going to go let them know."

Paige turns back to me. "Are you dating anyone?"

I scratch the back of my neck, looking away, embarrassed. Paige knows my whole sorry story—I dated Cara for years, and we double-dated with Garrett and Paige through the whole thing. She saw everything practically firsthand. Me falling hopelessly in love. My proposal. The wedding plans. The invitations going out. Cara breaking up with me just two weeks before the I do's.

The fact that Paige can see something different in me— enough to suspect I have feelings for someone new—feels like she can see how foolish I'm being. Like I'm just setting myself up for another fall that she and Garrett will witness. I really have to get Addi out of my mind. Cara is a good person. If she found me unworthy of marrying, it's probably wise for me to stay far away from any future relationships.

I turn as Garrett comes walking over, the Lewis & Clark Lanes employee at his side. As they pass by us, Garrett looks at Paige, motions to the back of the furthest lane, and says,

"We're going to go behind and get it!" with as much excitement as a ten-year-old about to go on his first rollercoaster.

I think Paige is going to press me for more information, but instead, she changes the subject. "Do you remember when Emmie was born, and I was trying to figure out life with a baby who cried nonstop and a toddler whose entire mission was to destroy the house?"

I chuckle. "I remember when Garrett would come to a site, he had new stories daily of things like finding the milk in the pantry and the cereal in the fridge."

Paige laughs, too. "I swear I couldn't even have told you what six plus three was for those first couple of months. With the amount of sleep I got with a baby like Emmie, my maternity leave was over way too soon."

"I bet."

"So one day, I was back at the hospital, working a twelve-hour shift, and I went into a patient's room to do all the discharge teaching. I told him he needed to be on a liquid diet for the next week, the name of the doctor he'd need to follow up with, what medications to take—all of it. The guy was just so happy the whole time, which is my favorite thing to see when I'm discharging a patient. Thirty minutes after I sent the man on his way, I found out that I had gone into the wrong patient's room."

"You sent the wrong guy home?"

Paige nods. "He'd been so happy because he thought that meant he didn't have to do the MRI he was dreading. All the information I'd given him—diet, doctor, medication, everything—was wrong."

She shakes her head at the memory, and we both chuckle.

"It was funny, sure, and we all had a laugh, including the patient I accidentally sent home and the one I was supposed to discharge. But as I went home that night, I just kept thinking about what could've happened if it had been a patient who had needed a lifesaving medication. Or one of a million other scenarios that could've been just as devastating. The list of ways it could've gone so wrong kept piling up in my head, keeping me awake all night long.

"The truth was, my sleep-deprived brain very well could have caused a major catastrophe. The thought sickened me. The next morning, I called my supervisor and let her know that I needed a longer leave, and I didn't go back for another five weeks."

"I never knew that was the reason why you decided to stay home longer. I figured it was because of Emmie."

She nods slowly. "I felt very damaged. I questioned whether I even deserved to be a nurse. I was embarrassed, and I asked Garrett not to say anything to anyone."

"I'm sorry."

She looks over my shoulder and smiles, so I turn to see Garrett coming out from the door leading behind the pin deck, holding his bowling ball over his head like it's a trophy and he just won the Super Bowl.

Then she meets my eyes again. "Do you think I should've quit after that? That it was too big a mistake for me to ever be a nurse again?"

"No!" Is she thinking about quitting? That feels so wrong. Being a nurse is so much of who Paige is. "You're amazing at what you do. Garrett tells me all the time about how much your patients and the entire hospital staff love you. It would be a tragedy if you let that one mistake define your entire career and choose to quit."

She meets my eyes for a long moment, and then says, "Right. Just like it would be a tragedy if you let one failed relationship define the rest of your life and keep you from developing a meaningful relationship with someone else."

Then she stands up to go congratulate her husband on his successful bowling ball retrieval, leaving me on the bench feeling like I just got hit with a semi-truck of truth that I'm not sure I'm ready to accept.

CHAPTER 10

Addison

I just finished a four-hour walk-in pantry job at a client's house and head back to the inn. The big jobs are the most satisfying, but the quick ones like this here and there are fun and give me the boost I need to tackle the big things.

And I have a massively huge job starting tomorrow. A client in a mansion in Lake Oswego wants me to organize both the husband's and wife's office spaces, a craft room, four bedroom closets, a toy room, and a family room. I plan to spend a full eight days at their house. I've already met with the client to assess and make a list of all the organization products we'll need to accomplish the monumental task. I ordered them from my favorite supplier, but the shipment was delayed, and I've been worried it won't arrive in time.

But I got a text that all the boxes were delivered to the inn just before I left my client's house. I can't wait to open them and get everything organized to start on the house tomorrow morning.

Not only is organizing the supplies one of my favorite parts but getting everything ready before starting is essential to the job going as smoothly as a job that large can go. I even grab lunch at a drive-through in Gresham so I can get started the moment I step foot into the inn. With as much as I ordered, it'll probably take every table in the dining room to get it all sorted.

I spot Ian's truck in his driveway even before I'm around the bend in the road enough to see the inn's sign, and I smile. Sure, the truck means he's home, which means he's close to my place, but it's not like I'm going to see him. So I'm really just grinning over seeing his truck. Ridiculous. I shake my head as I turn off the road and onto the inn's long driveway.

The fact that I can't find a parking space in my own eight-car parking lot is my first clue that a lot is going on at the inn. Still, I'm not quite prepared for the chaos I find when I open the front door.

All the boxes of supplies—all twenty-eight of them—are stacked in the lobby. Two little kids dressed like monkeys, who look like they're probably three or four, are pounding their plastic dinosaurs on the terrain of the multi-level box tower. I have no idea who the kids are, so I just wave and say hi. The loudest sounds are coming from the gathering room, so I walk to the left and poke my head in the double-wide doorway.

Bex must be filming her *Sterling Sisters* segment because she and all four of her sisters are seated in a semi-circle, each one talking before the previous one quite finishes. All of her sisters' kids who aren't old enough to go to school are running around the room, laughing and squealing and screaming, like they're trying to prove that their mom and aunts can stay cool amid chaos.

Interestingly enough, it doesn't explain who the kids playing dinosaur on my boxes are. Movement from the opposite side of the lobby—beyond the doorway to the kitchen and dining area—catches my attention. I leave the chaos of the gathering room, step over all the boxes and little kids dressed as monkeys in the lobby, and head to, hopefully, a more serene kitchen.

The room is so full of people and things that it takes a moment to make sense of what I'm seeing. Every single table in the room is filled with something, and four kids and half a dozen adults are all moving nonstop at the end of the room opposite the kitchen area. From the kitchen, Peyton waves, flashes her bright smile, and calls out, "I can't stop stirring, but come over."

Bewildered, I head back to the kitchen end of the room. Peyton holds her arm out—the one that isn't currently whisking some kind of sauce on the stove—and gives me a hug. "A little crazy in here, huh? I am making a week's worth of meals for a family of six because tomorrow morning the mom is going into the hospital to have a baby—child number five, if you can believe it. And if anyone needs a week's worth of meals already prepared, it's them, for sure."

A week's worth of food for six people. With the kinds of meals Peyton prepares, it makes sense that every burner on the stove has a pot on it, and every bit of counter space is taken up with food, cutting boards, and bowls of things in progress. The big dining table we eat on is filled with food containers, all with their lids neatly next to them, all of them labeled, some of them filled.

"And Timini?" I ask, motioning to the other end of the room.

"Oh, remember that client who was doing the extravagant production of *The Wizard of Oz* for preschoolers? They wanted a photo shoot of the kids wearing the costumes Timini made. And, of course, there are a ton of last-minute alterations. She's even had to sew an emergency lion's tail. She's so fast, it's unbelievable.

"Anyway, that's why her sewing machines and fabric are everywhere. The woman in the yellow shirt is the client, and the one in navy is the photographer. Obviously, I mean she's the one with the camera. The other three are moms of the kiddos."

Timini is helping to get four kids and a dog—Dorothy, Tin Man, Scarecrow, the Cowardly Lion, and Toto—looking perfect, while the photographer and the client are attempting to pose them and the moms are trying to get them to stay put and not be distracted by the dog that's yapping like it's trying to narrate a high-speed car chase. Timini definitely has her hands full. With how introverted she is, when this is all over, she's going to crash like a toddler on the car ride home from a playground after being hopped up on sugar, sunshine, and friends for too long.

"What about you?" Peyton asks as she moves the sauce off the burner and starts cutting some vegetables. "What's on your schedule for the rest of the day?"

I glance toward the lobby, then race forward and catch

Dorothy's basket that one of the kids from the photo shoot threw, saving the container of mashed potatoes on the table it's heading for. I toss it back to Timini, who seems to notice me for the first time and calls out, "Thank you!"

Then I turn back to Peyton. "I need to open all those boxes in the lobby and get everything organized. Some pieces will need to be put together, and then they all need to be grouped by which day I'll need them."

Peyton grimaces. "Well, at least the lobby's still available."

I nod. There's a free room upstairs where I plan to put everything, but it isn't big enough to open and assemble all twenty-eight boxes of supplies and still have room to organize. So really, the lobby is my only option.

When I get back to the boxes, the two monkeys are climbing on them like, well, monkeys, and the boxes probably aren't strong enough to hold them. So I convince them that empty boxes are more fun for their dinosaurs and hand them the cardboard boxes as I open them. And I'm right—the cardboard boxes *are* more fun. Fun enough that the half-dozen I've handed over to the kids have drawn in the six kids from Bex's family and the other four kids from the photo shoot.

Apparently, the lobby is also the "staging area" for the photo shoot, so before long, we're joined by the moms of the photo shoot kids and a whole lot of noise. Everyone is trying to direct kids and adults alike, even though no one can really hear what anyone is saying. The louder this group gets, the louder Bex and her sisters in the other room get, trying to be heard over the din.

The lobby is so full that I don't even have space to open another box. I worry that if I start carrying things upstairs, all the chaos will follow me, so I do my best to step over kids and boxes to get to the items I've already opened and move them to the top of the check-in counter.

All of it happens to the tune of kids shouting and making dinosaur, monkey, lion, scarecrow, and tin man sounds, adults directing, and cardboard boxes shuffling. Then I stack the unopened boxes in a tall, even pile, so they don't resemble a mountain terrain or steps—hopefully making them less enticing to climb on.

I cross my fingers that all the supplies in the boxes will be safe, then take the first opening in the crowd to escape down the hallway toward the back door and head outside.

As soon as the door closes behind me, most of the noise disappears, and I collapse against the stone wall of the inn, feeling like I just escaped from a stampede at the zoo. I guess I should've expected this when I found my roommates at a Creative Women Entrepreneurs seminar in a group of women who run their businesses from home.

I glance across the beautifully mowed grass to the always-open gate separating the inn's yard from Ian's, and I suddenly want nothing more than to go through that gate and see if he's in his shop. From what I've noticed, he's gone to sites three or four days a week, and on the weekdays that he's home, he's usually working in his shop.

But no. That's a very bad idea. I need to keep my distance and focus on something else. Like the weeds in the flower beds that need pulling or the blackberry bushes that are encroaching along the back fence.

Because somewhere along the way, I've realized that I'm not ready to open myself to a new relationship for more reasons than just worrying it could be a rebound. I'm also not ready for the probable rejection. To let a guy know that I like him only to be turned away. I've experienced it way too many times in the ten years I've been dating, and it's painful every time.

It hits me then that the underlying reason why I broke up with Matthew was rejection. He didn't reject dating me or even becoming an item. His rejection was more subtle, so I hadn't recognized it. But he rejected me every time I wanted to do anything that would progress our relationship into something less casual. Or do something outside of our usual takeout Tuesdays and Saturday afternoon hike or bike ride followed by a movie. He rejected my wanting to build a life with him. Or spending more time with him, talking about life goals together, or even just talking more.

Then, while eating Tuesday takeout one day, instead of talking about what we were going to do on Saturday like always, I told Matthew I needed to buy a new coffee table and asked if he wanted to go shopping with me that Thursday. A *Thursday*, of all days. Apparently, either coffee tables or Thursdays were Matthew's kryptonite, because he said we were going too fast, that he wasn't ready, and that he didn't know when he ever would be. After two years of dating, seeing me a third time in a single week to shop for a coffee table was moving things too quickly.

So, in the end, it was the constant rejection that made me break things off with him. And now, standing in my back-yard, I know I'm not ready to face that again. Weeds and blackberry bushes are definitely the better option. I march right over to some nearby weeds and yank them out just to prove my point. The goal right now is to figure out what I want in life and decide if moving to Quicksand and starting my own business was the right thing to do. My goal is not to become interested in my neighbor.

But as I pull more and more weeds, I keep seeing Ian's shop from the corner of my eye, and I start to wonder what it looks like inside.

And, okay, maybe what he looks like as he works inside.

He's probably wearing a t-shirt, and those muscles I saw when he was mowing are probably straining his t-shirt as he works.

With as much care as he seems to put into everything I've witnessed him do, he's probably crafting beautiful things that are practically works of art. And his eyes are probably there, looking amazing and amused, and waiting to draw me in and make me forget how to form sentences.

Before I even realize what's happening, I'm through the gate separating our yards and halfway to his shed. Maybe it wouldn't be so bad to stop in and see him. After all, I haven't been stalking Matthew on social media, haven't thought about what he might think of me dating again, and haven't hoped he'd send me a text letting me know how he's doing. So I'm good. No rebound issues at all.

I hear the sound of a saw for a moment before it shuts off, so I raise my hand to knock on the door, imagining the moment he opens it, a smile spread across that beautiful face, and my heart practically floats.

Then I picture what his face would look like if he didn't

want to see me, and my heart feels like fragile glass plummeting toward the ground, about to shatter. I change my mind. This really is a very bad idea. I turn around without knocking and head straight for the gate to escape back into my own yard.

CHAPTER 11
Ian

I SHUT off my bandsaw and am brushing the sawdust off a beautiful piece of oak when I think I hear something. A quiet knock? Just footsteps? Maybe my subconscious picked up on a shadow or something because I suddenly feel like someone's at my shop door. It's probably nothing, but I head to the door anyway.

When I open it, I see Addi walking away, and she's almost at the gate to her yard. "Addi!" She turns around, and from the blush on her cheeks, I guess she might've been at my door but left without knocking. "Want to come in?"

She glances toward her house before looking back in my direction. She's clearly still hesitating. But she walked all the way to my shed, so at least part of her wants to come in. And a big part of me really wants her to. I push the door open all the way so if that part wins out, she'll have a clear path.

She shakes her head and chuckles as she walks toward

me. "You, Ian, must have supersonic hearing. I swear I didn't make a sound coming up to your door."

I shrug. "What can I say? It's my superpower." It's not my superpower. Especially because all the noise from the saw I just ran is still making my ears ring. But claiming that is better than admitting what might've actually happened—that so much of my focus is on her at all times I can practically sense her nearness.

"Welcome to my shop," I say, motioning to it all. Addi walks slowly around the space, looking at everything as she goes, her eyes seeming to fall on each thing without missing any. I'm suddenly dying to know what thoughts are going through her head.

"It's different than your grandpa's shop. More… airy."

I nod. "I had to tear his old shop down and rebuild before I could move my equipment here—it wasn't up to code anymore. That back wall, though, is finished with all the wood from his shop, and everything hanging on it is from my grandpa." It's the best part of the space. My grandpa taught me so much every summer that the man deserves an entire wall as a shrine. By the way Addi smiles while taking in all the details, she agrees.

She asks for a tour, so I show her everything. I figure she's just asking to be polite, but when she asks more questions about everything, I start telling her about the names of every saw, sander, and tool.

"I never knew you were interested in this kind of stuff."

She lifts a shoulder in a shrug, and it makes me notice just how great her shoulders are.

"Back in Amarillo, I designed storage solutions, and I

worked closely with our manufacturing plant. We mostly made our pieces out of plastics—the kinds of things you'd find at Target or Bed, Bath and Beyond, so it was basically nothing at all like what you do here. It's just interesting to see the difference between that and what you use for wood-working." She runs her fingers along the piece of wood I cut moments before she showed up at my door. "Your finished product is a million times prettier. What are you making with this?"

She jumps up to sit on the counter at the end of my shop. I figure it means she really wants to hear, so I talk about the fireplace I'm designing for a remodel and explain the parts I assemble in my shop and the parts I do during installation at the client's home.

And she listens the whole time. I try to think of the last time I've had a captive audience like this, and I can't come up with one. My grandma listens, of course, but she already knows pretty much everything there is to know about carpentry from my grandpa, so I never get to talk to her about it like this. Cara definitely never wanted to know anything about my job. Ever. She wanted me to have a good job with steady pay—she didn't want to have to hear about it. That was stuff I was supposed to chat about with my "carpentry friends." Having Addi listen is new. It's nice.

When I finish telling her all about it, she says, "Play Rapid Fire with me."

That's a game I haven't played since that summer when I was fourteen. I cock my head. "You offering anything?"

Addison looks up, like she's trying to think of anything she can offer, but then shakes her head.

"Awesome. Double Rapid Fire it is." I was hoping she didn't have anything to offer in payment for a one-sided game because I really want to hear her answers, too. I sit on the worktable across from Addi, an aisle separating us.

"One, two, three," Addi says, as we bounce our fists on our thighs. Then she makes scissors with her hand and I make paper. She's less predictable than she was as a kid. "Yes!" she says. "Okay, last serious relationship—how long ago, and how serious?"

"Wow, Addi. Just like when you were a kid, you jump into the hard questions."

"Sorry. Want to use a skip?"

"Nope. It's okay." I don't exactly want to talk about it, but I also want her to know. "Lasted just over a year, ended two weeks before you moved in. It was pretty serious. I thought we'd get married." I hold back my own flinch saying it and am surprised that Addi's face doesn't hold distaste at hearing it. In fact, all I can see is curiosity, like something just clicked into place, and something else I can't quite place. Not pity. Understanding, maybe?

"Two years for me, also ended two weeks before I moved in, went nowhere."

Interesting. We both had relationships that ended at virtually the same time. Maybe that was where the understanding came from. But now I'm the curious one. I expect her to ask a follow-up question—since she won the round, she gets to ask first. She must see my reluctance to talk about it because she doesn't ask.

Unless she doesn't want to open herself up to me asking a follow-up to hers. Fair enough.

She wins the next rock, paper, scissors battle, too, and asks, "On a scale of one to ten, how much do you love your job?"

"Eight." The point of the game is to answer fast, without giving yourself a chance to think. My answer kind of surprises me.

"Eight," she answers for herself as well. Then she says, "Huh. With as much as you light up when talking about it, I would've guessed a nine or ten."

She wins the next round. I need to switch up my rock, paper, scissors strategy. "If you could give up one aspect of your job, what would it be?"

"Trim."

"Bead collections."

I finally win a round and ask, "What's the part of your job you like the best?"

"Finding creative solutions to problems that seem impossible to solve."

"Building things."

Then I win again and ask, "What would make your job a ten?"

"Owning my own organization design business."

I'm dying to ask her about it, but I have to answer first. That's the rule. "Owning my own custom cabinet shop."

Her eyebrows shoot up and her mouth opens like she's about to ask me something, but since I asked the question, I get to ask a follow-up question first. Also the rules. "I want to hear more about this design business."

"I love helping people to organize the spaces in their homes. I really do. There are just so many times that I think of a storage solution that would be perfect—if it actually existed. If I still worked at my old job, I would've made a mockup and really pushed for it in our production meetings.

"Back then, though, I wasn't in people's homes so much, organizing their spaces, so I didn't have the practical knowledge I've gotten from being in the field. I'd love to combine both. And with my own shop, I would have that kind of freedom."

Everything about her comes alive as she talks about it. Happiness and excitement fill her expressions and her tone of voice. Her sense of adventure was what first made me want to become friends with her when I was eleven—I love that she hasn't lost that. I want to have those adventures with her again. And I want all those big dreams of hers to come true.

"Now, I want to hear about your custom cabinets because, Ian, that's perfect! I can totally picture you doing that. Would you run it out of this shop?"

I shake my head. "It's too small. About all I can make here is one built-in at a time. I would need a shop large enough to build several sets of cabinets at the same time and have space for some employees. So it'll take time, but all the decisions I make as a subcontractor are aiming me toward that goal."

I haven't shared that dream with anyone. It feels great to say it out loud and to have someone hear it. Especially someone who seems so interested and believes I can do it. I hadn't guessed how great that would feel. Like a helium balloon in my chest.

"If you start doing custom storage cabinets for parts of

the home other than kitchens—like mudrooms, storage areas, laundry rooms, things like that—let me know. I have several clients who I bet would love to have you build them some."

No words come out of my mouth. I just sit, looking at Addi. I haven't had a ton of experience with serious relationships other than Cara, and with her, support only went one way. She never would've offered to give my name to potential clients. I thought Cara and I had a pretty perfect relationship. But the more time I spend around Addi, the more I realize that maybe I'd been romanticizing our relationship. Maybe it wasn't all I'd thought it was.

I become aware that I've just been staring at Addi when she shifts her gaze to the floor. I lean forward a bit. "Thank you." I hope my words come out as heartfelt as I mean them.

She meets my eyes, a look in hers that I haven't seen before. I don't know what it is, exactly—all I know is that I want to reach out and touch that earnest, beautiful face. Then I glance at her lips and realize how badly I want to pull her close and kiss those lips.

There's a good three feet of aisle separating us, but when she leans forward, I know she must be feeling it, too.

Her shift in hand placement made her push down on the edge of a board that hung over the counter's edge. It flips it up, sending both it and the container of one-inch-long wooden dowels resting on it flying. The board clatters to the ground and the dowels scatter to the floor, rolling everywhere.

We both jump off our seats on the work surfaces pretty quickly, and Addi's hands fly to her mouth. Then she mumbles, "Oh my goodness. This is blueberries all over again."

I chuckle. "Nah. Nothing like blueberries. Which is good because I like this shirt."

Her eyes fly to my chest, and my pecs may involuntarily flex, which is closely followed by her face reddening and mine breaking into a grin. She grabs the empty container from where it has rolled right next to my drill press, and I take it from her and set it on the counter next to me. "It's okay, Addi. Not a big deal."

She grabs the container back and bends down to pick up the dowels. "There isn't a surly man in deli to call for clean-up on the front aisle, so it's the least I can do."

I smile and crouch next to her, picking up the little round pieces of wood that have spread themselves everywhere. As we work side by side, our knees, arms, and sometimes hands brushing each other, all I want to do is turn toward her, cradle her face in my hands, and kiss her until we both forget about the spilled dowels.

Addi looks over at me with her face so open and beautiful, and I nearly do just that. But then her eyes shift to how far the mess has spread behind me, and I look, too. As much as I want to kiss her, the mess tells me I can't. It's like the universe is showing me a physical representation of the mess I'd make of things with Addi if I did, and I like her way too much to do that to her.

CHAPTER 12

Addison

I HEAD HOME from a half-day job in Gresham, wishing I had a job lined up to take the other half of the day. It's still scary having my own business and knowing that a paycheck isn't going to magically appear from a company anymore, so gaps in my schedule make me nervous. I have another half day unscheduled next week and two the week after that. Sure, I might get more clients in time to fill them, but I can't guarantee it.

As soon as I open the front door, Bex comes running from the dining room, phone in hand, looking like she's simultaneously going to hold her arms up in a V while running a victory lap and pull at her hair in desperation. "Adds! I'm so glad you're home! I was literally just pressing on your contact to call you. Are you off for the rest of the day?" When I nod, she says, "Oh good. I need a giant favor from you, and I promise I will let you cash in on that favor at any moment of any day."

The sounds of kids eating, laughing, arguing, and telling jokes all at the same time are coming from the kitchen, and it's all I can do to keep my attention on Bex and not walk in there to see what's up.

"Remember how I've been dying to get an interview with Steve Stonebreaker for my channel for months? I just got a call from his publicist—he's in Portland and has an opening. Today! But there's no school today, and I already told my sister I would watch her kids, so they're here, and I can't take them with me. Adds, you have to help me. I can't pass up this chance."

"You want me to watch your sister's kids?"

"Yes. Thank you! Seriously, I owe you big time. Peyton is doing that big catering thing until late tonight, and Timini isn't back from visiting her parents until tomorrow. I already cleared it with my sister, and she's good to have you watch them instead."

"Bex, I don't know how to take care of kids! I have one sister who is two years younger than me, so it's been forever since she was a kid, and I have zero nieces and nephews. I wouldn't even know what to do!"

Bex brushes away my comment with her hand as she goes to the check-in counter and starts filling her oversized bag with things she keeps in the drawer, placing her video equipment on top. "It's seriously not hard. There are only four of them, and they're good kids. It'll be a piece of cake. It's an hour drive there and an hour back, and probably an hour for the interview, so I'll be gone three hours, tops."

She finishes packing her bag and looks at me. "Just take

them to the park or something." She holds up a set of keys. "My sister traded me vehicles, and I can trade you, so you'll have her Yukon with the car seats for the younger ones. She keeps it stocked with wipes and a first aid kit and everything else you could possibly need."

Panic rises in me more and more by the second.

Bex sets the keys on the counter and says, "These are for the Yukon," and then grabs my keys right out of my hand. She gives me a hug and a quick "You're the best!" before poking her head into the dining area. "Addison is going to watch you all until I get back. She's awesome, and I know you'll all be angels for her." Then she races out the door.

Before I've even taken a step toward the kitchen, Bex opens the front door again and pokes her head in. "Oh, and watch out for Drew. He has even less stranger danger than the rest of them." Then she's gone again.

Shock keeps me from moving a single inch from the spot where I stand for a good thirty seconds. Then, I hear shouting over whose carrot stick someone just took a bite out of was whose, and I rush into the dining area to hopefully quell whatever is going on. Four kids sit at the dining table, and two of them are having a tug-of-war over a carrot stick. The other two are using their carrot sticks for a mini sword fight. The moment they see me, all four put down their carrots and smile at me like they have actual halos over their heads.

"Hi," I say, giving a little wave. "I'm Addison, and I guess we're going to hang out today."

The oldest kid shrugs, picks up his sandwich, and takes a

bite. The two youngest go back to sword-fighting, and the remaining girl just grins at me. So I take a seat facing the girl.

"Do you mind introducing me to everyone?"

"No problem." The girl points to her older brother. "That's Ash. He's eight, but just barely. He's the oldest, so he thinks he's the smartest. I'm Beth. I'm six and the one that's *actually* the smartest."

She flinches when Ash's carrot stick hits her in the arm but keeps going like nothing happened. "That's Chelle. She's five, and the one sticking the carrot up his nose is Drew. He's four." She reaches out and yanks the carrot stick from her youngest sibling's nose. "If you forget, you can just call us A, B, C, and D," she says, pointing to each of them in order.

"Clever." I try not to let the shock of being in charge of four kids who are all basically a year apart in age show on my face.

"But it's like secret cleverness," Beth says, leaning in and cupping her hand at the side of her mouth conspiratorially, "because our actual names—Dasher, Elizabeth, Michelle, and Andrew—aren't alphabetical at all. Only our nicknames are."

"Extra clever."

The younger two switch from sword-fighting and nose-sticking their carrots to throwing them, and it only takes about one-fourth of a second for the older two to join in. "Okay," I say, standing up, "it looks like maybe you're done with lunch. Want to go to the park?"

They all give their yeses in the form of fist-pumping, jumping up and down, ear-splitting shouting of words I can't even make out, and, in Chelle's case, dancing.

"Let's, um, get lunch cleaned up, and then we'll head out."

They throw all their garbage away like the trash can is a basketball hoop and they're in a slam dunk competition. They're all wearing shoes and look like they're probably ready to go. Thankfully, it occurs to me to ask if anyone needs to go to the bathroom before we leave.

Even though they were mostly ready, it still takes a full fifteen minutes to get them all outside to the Yukon and hop in. And then back in. And then back out. It's like we're playing a game of whack-a-mole where one of them keeps popping up outside of the vehicle every time I get another one in.

Eventually, all four are buckled into their correct seats, and all the doors are closed. As I go around to the driver's side of the vehicle, I stop at the back and lean against it just to catch my breath.

"Looks like you're having a party over there."

At the sound of Ian's voice, my attention flies to where his truck is parked at the end of his driveway, just twenty feet away. It's been a week and a half since we came so close to kissing, and I still think about it daily and long for a moment like it to return. But right now, I long for some help even more.

"Ian! Please tell me you have absolutely nothing going on in your life for the next little bit and have been hoping someone would come along and ask you to spend an afternoon at the park."

He smiles that amused smile he seems to have reserved

just for me that's getting way too much use. "Where'd you get all the kids?"

"They're Bex's nephews and nieces, and she begged me to watch them for the afternoon. Do you have any experience with kids?"

"Sure—all my brothers have kids, and I love hanging out with them. Plus, I host my Junior Woodworkers club every week."

"Ian, please help me. I don't have any experience, and I don't know if I can survive this on my own."

I jolt in surprise as something hits the window just behind me, and I turn to see that an all-out stuffed animal war is going on in the back seats. I hadn't even seen stuffed animals in the vehicle. But Ian is walking toward me, either out of morbid curiosity or because he's willing to help. Hopefully, it's the latter.

"Bex says it'll be a piece of cake, and that they're angels."

"Clearly, she's right."

"Of course, if you gave thirty kindergartners unlimited snow cones and cotton candy and then put them in a room together and asked Bex to play a game with them, she'd emerge an hour later saying it was a piece of cake, that they were angels, and that she wants to do it again soon."

Ian glances toward his shop.

"Do you have a lot of work that has to get done today? If you do, you can tell me no. I'll survive it on my own." I mean, I'm pretty sure I will. I glance at the kids. Okay, I'm maybe five percent sure.

He looks at his shop for a long moment, and then he turns back to me. "Nothing I can't get done later tonight."

"So you'll come with me?"

He nods, and I have to stop myself from throwing my arms around him to show my overflowing, can't-contain-it, have-to-show-it gratitude. I stop fighting it and give him a quick hug before I can decide it's a bad idea, then run around to my side of the Yukon. We need to leave before the little ninjas inside the vehicle find a way to escape and I have to start the process of getting them buckled in all over again.

Once we get to the biggest park in town and all the kids run squealing in excitement toward it, I let out a huge breath of relief that I no longer have to keep them contained. But it doesn't take long before I've used a handful of wipes, half a dozen squirts of hand sanitizer, two bandages from the first aid kit, an extra pair of socks from the bag in the car, made three trips with kids to the bathroom, caught Drew trying to escape four times, and asked the kids not to show me any snails, snakes, beetles, squirrels, or slugs they find. And better yet, not to pick them up at all.

Right now, the kids are all together, huddling under one of the platforms leading up to the slides, talking with some other kids they've made friends with since we've been here. It's the first time they're all within sight at the same time and no one needs to go to the bathroom. I collapse on a bench next to Ian.

"Thank you again for coming. I don't know how I could've gotten through this without you. Seriously—I can't even imagine the shenanigans they could've gotten into each time I took one to the bathroom or went to the car for a bandage."

"You say that as though we've already gotten through it,

but I'm pretty sure they're having a war council as we speak."

"As long as they let me sit here next to you for thirty seconds right now, I'm okay to let that be a problem for future me."

From where we've both flopped down on the bench, our hands are next to each other, our fingers bumping. Ian moves his pinky finger, running it along the edge of my hand. I close my eyes and let myself feel every single thrill of goose bumps that go all the way up my arm and to my heart. Maybe he really is feeling the same things I am.

Ever since Ian told me how recent his breakup was and how serious it had been, I've tried not to push him. Fear has stopped me plenty, too. But I'm falling for him—more so every single time I see him.

I'm in the middle of imagining what it would be like if he ran those fingertips of his all the way up my arm when I hear breathing next to my other ear and my eyes fly open. "I know you said no bugs, snakes, or… I can't remember what else," the five-year-old Chelle says, "but this isn't any of those. Check out this frog I found!" She plops the big-bellied thing down on my arm, and it lets out a big *Crooooak!* at the same time that I scream.

Chelle grimaces as it hops away. "So… No frogs, either?"

"Pretty please?" I beg.

"Check," Chelle says, drawing an invisible checkmark in the air with her finger. "No more frogs." She's halfway back to the slide when she turns back. "Tadpoles aren't frogs, right? Because I think there's a pond back there."

"I think we better say no to tadpoles and no to going to the pond," Ian says.

Chelle writes another invisible check, then turns to the others under the platform and shouts, "The tadpole plan is out, guys!"

I bury my face in my hands and mumble, "How much more time do we have?"

"Until Bex's three hours are up? Um, it looks like about fifteen minutes."

That's worth taking my hands off my face for. "Oh, thank heavens. So, we can head back now, right?"

Ian smiles the sweetest smile at me, and then he reaches out and gives my hand a squeeze before standing up. His hand is only on mine for a second, but it sends such a jolt of electricity through me that I think I might be able to handle the monumental task of getting all four kids back in the vehicle.

I can't help but check Ian out as he brings all of the kids together for a huddle and pulls me into it, talking to the kids like he's the quarterback explaining to the team what the next play is. Then he rallies them to grab any shoes that somehow fell off, water bottles that have been tossed aside, and anything else they left, and we all head back to the Yukon. He's so cute with them that I could watch all day. Remarkably, they all listen and head to the vehicle.

Getting them inside it is another story. I've never seen so much opening doors, running around to the other side, closing doors, opening again, and running around again. And it's coming from all the kids and in all different directions. If it were a choreographed show on Broadway, I'd still be impressed.

Ash and Beth are giggling on the opposite side of the SUV from me. I almost walk around to ask them to get in, but before I can, Drew takes off running at full speed toward the playground. No sooner does Ian run after him than Chelle takes off in the direction of the pond, so I chase her down. By the time we get them both back to the vehicle, I want to kiss Ash and Beth. They're both in their seats, seatbelts on, actually looking like angels.

And they even stay there while Ian and I get Chelle and Drew buckled in. I let out a huge breath as I get into the driver's seat and start the Yukon.

Ian motions to the clock in the console. "With as long as that took, Bex will probably beat us back to the inn."

"Music to my ears," I whisper as I pull out of the parking space.

A few minutes into the drive, I realize this is the quietest the kids have been since the moment Bex left me with them. It's quiet enough that I can even hear the radio—I hadn't even realized it had been turned on this whole time. All that's coming from them now are whispers and giggles.

Ian must notice at the same time, because he says, "You all sure are being quiet."

There's more giggling, and definitely more whispering and "*Shh*"s coming from them.

At a stop sign, I glance at Ian. "Maybe we just wore them out?"

Ian twists to look at the kids, then turns back and mumbles only loud enough for me to hear, "Or this is the calm before the storm, and they're about to carry out those plans they made in their council of war earlier."

I look at him in alarm. "No. It can't be that."

Ian looks out the window, squinting at something in the distance, not meeting my eyes. "Yeah, I'm sure it's fine." He reaches over and gives my knee a gentle squeeze, which isn't quite the comforting gesture he's probably meaning it to be. Especially when he adds, in a voice I don't believe at all, "We've got nothing to worry about."

CHAPTER 13

Ian

THE KIDS in the back seat keep up the whispering the whole ride home. That part is nice. And they've kept calm enough that I've been able to marvel at Addi. She may not have experience, and she may not have been planning on this today, but she's been such a trooper. Especially in taking care of kids as rambunctious as these. I can tell that she's exhausted, but she's still giving me the cutest smiles whenever she feels my gaze on her.

Today isn't what I had been planning on, either. But I wouldn't trade the past three hours with Addi for anything. As chaotic as it has been, it has also been… magical. It has shown me how much I like working with Addi. How much I like partnering with her.

I glance back at the kids. Whispering is fine—it's the giggling that worries me. I actually love it when my nieces and nephews giggle about some secret plans they've made. But I have a feeling these kids aren't giggling because they've drawn a smiley face on the inside bottom of my plastic cup of punch at a family party or because they've hidden their plastic insect toys like Easter eggs throughout the house.

Addi pulls into the circular drive in front of the inn. Unfortunately, her car—the one that Bex is driving—isn't parked in the lot. As all the kids unbuckle their seat belts and start climbing out, Addi turns to me. "Thank you again for coming with me. Is there anything in your shop I can do that will help you make up for the time you lost today? I could come over as soon as Bex gets here."

I glance out the window. Instead of the kids running off in all directions and having to be herded back into the house like I expected, they're all in a cluster at the back of the vehicle. "I don't think you better say goodbye to me yet. We might want to hold off on all plans until Bex is here."

Addi must catch some concern in my voice or expression because she looks at the pack of kids at the back of the vehicle, worry and wariness all over her face. When we get out of the SUV and walk around to them, they're lined up with their backs against the vehicle, hands behind them, grinning like they've never been more proud of themselves.

"Look what we brought back with us," Beth says, and all four of the kids motion like they're Vanna White, presenting a young boy who's standing in the middle of their group. He's one of the friends they'd made at the park who'd been present at their war council under the slides.

Addi's gasp is audible, and her hands fly to her mouth.

These kids are even more ingenious than I gave them credit for.

"His name is Jaxon," Drew says. "We're friends now. He wanted to come over and play."

"So we planned everything." Chelle throws her arms wide. "Aren't we the best at planning? You guys didn't even know we did it!"

"And we even got the timing perfect," Ash says, puffing his chest out. "Drew and Chelle took off running so you'd chase them, which gave us all the time we needed to get Jaxon hidden under the blanket in the back."

"And I stayed quiet the whole time!" Jaxon looks so proud of himself for that feat.

These kids pulled it off like pros. They probably have a bright future ahead of them as actors, business strategists, or criminal masterminds.

Addi starts breathing fast and pacing in a small circle. "I can't believe I just kidnapped a kid! His mom is probably running around frantic, searching for him. The police are going to come, they're going to arrest me, and I'm going to jail for kidnapping."

"It's going to be okay." I take a step toward her and place my hand gently on her shoulder.

"No, it's not. We have a kidnapped kid right here! What do we do? Do we take him back to the park and say sorry? What if they're already out searching?"

I pull out my phone and say, "Let's see what the police want us to do," as I dial 9-1-1. Because Addi's so panicked, I wrap an arm around her shoulder. She turns into me, and I hug her to my chest as well as I can while holding the phone to my ear.

"Nine-one-one. What's your emergency?"

"We want to report an accidental kidnapping. We were babysitting some kids and took them to the park. As we were packing up to leave, they very expertly snuck a new friend into the vehicle when we weren't looking and hid him under some blankets."

"Can you describe the child for me?"

"Um, yeah. He looks like he's about five."

"I'm six!"

"Correction—he's six, and his name is Jaxon. He's got brown hair and a green shirt."

"Which park was he abducted from?"

I flinch at the use of the word *abducted*. "Pioneer. Listen, I swear this was an accident. Well, accidental on our part. It was very purposeful on the kids' part."

"Pioneer Park. Okay, it sounds like another operator is talking to his very alarmed mother right now."

"Do you want us to drive him back there?" All the kids are racing around to the backyard, and Addi is chasing after them, so I follow.

"No. We have officers on their way to your location right now."

"Perfect. Thank you." I hang up, grateful that we don't have to try and get all five kids back into the vehicle, and I help Addi get them all back to the front yard. That way, when the police come, we won't have to explain how we just lost the kid we kidnapped along with the ones we were babysitting.

The first officer must've been close by because he's there in minutes. Before long, there are four police cars, all with their lights on, pulled in from both sides of the circular driveway, surrounding the Yukon. I didn't even know Quicksand had that many police officers on duty at once. Right behind them, the local news station, who must've been listening to the police scanners, pulls in and starts filming.

The officers split up, one asking me questions, one asking Addi, one asking Jaxon, and one asking the kids we're babysitting, probably checking to see if our stories match up. While my officer takes notes on what I say, I can hear Addi talking to hers.

"No—we didn't kidnap the other kids, too! They're the nieces and nephews of my roommate Bex Sterling. She was supposed to watch them today but then had an interview in Portland, and let me just call her. She can confirm."

As soon as the guy interviewing me—a balding man with his hair cut close who looks like he's in his early thirties—starts asking more questions, I can't focus on Addi any longer. Until she grabs hold of my arm and I turn to see a horrified expression on her face, her eyes wide, her phone still up to her ear.

"Bex is still in Portland! She's not finished, so she's probably still an hour and a half from being home."

I wrap my arms around her like she's just gotten in a car accident and is going into shock. "We'll make it."

Luckily, Jaxon's mom comes speeding into the driveway not long after, skidding to a stop behind the police cars. She gets out and runs to Jaxon. He eventually manages to wiggle out of her smothering hugs long enough to introduce her to his new friends and to ask if they can play again tomorrow.

If nothing else, Jaxon's words to his mom assure the police officers and the reporter that the events of the day were unintentional by all adult parties involved. Whatever excitement the reporter thought they were going to be a part of isn't exactly national news-worthy, so they don't stick around for long.

This entire afternoon has given me a lot of time to witness how Addi handles everything. Her nerves are frayed and she's stressed and exhausted, but she never took it out on the kids. I'm impressed.

I'm even more impressed by her bravery when she suggests we go into the house and make cookies. Which, of course, makes a huge mess and leaves two adults and four kids with shirts covered in flour and one with melted chocolate chips all around his mouth and cheeks. But the kids are quiet for a solid five minutes while they scarf down their confections.

I take the moment to put an arm around Addi and let her rest her head against my chest. She smells like strawberry lemonade, and I soak it in. I soak in every bit of the feel of her against me. I may have thought I could keep myself away from Addi before, but no longer. Not after today. Now, I want nothing more than to be near her.

Nearly five hours after she left, Bex bursts into the house with apologies and professions of undying gratitude and excitement over her incredible day. She barely sets her bags down when the kids' mom, Bex's sister, comes through the door. The kids emerge from the gathering room, where they'd been playing chase, all calm and full of smiles, looking as if they'd been angels the entire time.

While Bex is giving hugs to her nieces and nephews and saying goodbye, Addi grabs my hand and pulls me into the gathering room. Tired as I am, the feel of her hand in mine sends heat to my chest, and I know I'd follow her anywhere.

Luckily, where she leads me is to a couch, and I gladly collapse into it next to her.

"Did you ever think five hours could be so exhausting?"

I laugh and shake my head. "If you'd have asked me this morning what kinds of things were more tiring than taking care of kids for five hours, I could've easily listed a dozen. Now, though, I can't think of a single one."

Soon after we hear Bex's sister and the kids leave, Bex comes into the gathering room, holding a bag and a drink holder with two drinks. "I know that I still owe you both, big time, for watching the kids for me, and I will pay you back. But," she drags the word out as she puts the items on the table, "for now, this is an apology for taking so much longer than I thought. And for that whole thing with the police."

Addi leans forward, peeks into one of the bags, and her face lights up. "You brought us food from the Dragon's Chopstick?"

Bex nods, smiling. "And now, I'm going to leave you two in utter peace and quiet while I go upstairs. And leave you alone. With no one else home. Just the two of you."

Addi raises an annoyed eyebrow at Bex, and Bex holds up her hands. "Okay, okay, I get it. No one said that 'overdoing it' isn't my middle name."

As the sound of Bex's footsteps on the stairs fades, Addi looks at the bags of food, not moving. "Are you ever so tired that you wish you could just teleport yourself into bed? Well, right now, I wish I could teleport this food into my belly. I'm starving, but I think I'm too exhausted to even eat."

"I don't think I could ever be too exhausted to eat food from the Dragon's Chopstick. Lean back." I give her a little nudge backward, and she lets herself sink into the backrest of the couch. Then I pull all the items out of the bag and open each of the boxes. "Do you like sesame chicken?"

She nods, so I pick up a good-looking chunk of chicken with the chopsticks and bring it to Addi's waiting mouth. She closes her eyes as she chews it, and I just smile at her, loving the way her eyes crinkle at the sides, the way her smooth skin looks almost golden in the light of the early evening sun, making her cheekbones look so touchably soft. And the way her curls shine as they frame her face. Even after a day of stress and exhaustion, she's beautiful. How did I ever think I could keep from being attracted to her?

With her eyes still closed, she opens her mouth again, so I feed her another piece of chicken. Then she smiles before opening her eyes and looking at me. "I think you just saved my life by feeding me those two bites."

"So that's twice I've saved you today."

"You'll be getting your Medal of Honor in the mail any day now."

"No ceremony?" I take a bite of beef and broccoli, grateful for some meat since all I've eaten since breakfast is cookies.

"You have to save me three times for that."

"Duly noted."

After a few minutes of silence, where all our focus is on eating as a way to overcome our starvation and exhaustion, I say, "Do you want kids someday? Or did today ruin any chances of future Addi offspring?"

She gives a soft chuckle. "I think today would be effective birth control for anyone. But yeah. I do."

"Good. Because you're really great at it."

She gives me a look that I want to search for hours, trying to figure out what it all might mean. I only get a moment, though. It's enough to know that she appreciates the compliment.

"How about you?"

I've always wanted kids and jump at any chance I get to hang out with my nieces and nephews. But as crazy as today was, it has me thinking about how much I want kids of my own. After the way things ended with Cara, not only have I not allowed myself to think about it being a possibility, but the whole experience has left me questioning whether I'd ever be good enough.

All day long, though, as Addi and I took care of Ash, Beth, Chelle, and Drew, I haven't been able to stop imagining what life might be like with Addi. And that life has included kids of our own. Even through all the chaos of the day, I loved every moment of being with her. She's helping me heal. I don't want to be anywhere other than by her side.

I know the thoughts are dangerous, and I'll likely pay later for the hope they've raised that will be dashed, but right now, I don't care. I just want to live in that hope.

I nod. "I do, too."

Our eyes meet, and for a long moment, neither of us breaks eye contact. We just study each other, and I'd give anything to know what she's thinking. She's the one to finally break the connection. She grabs the box of Kung Pao Chicken, and while she's picking up a piece with her chopsticks, she says, "Thank you, again, for helping me through a rather memorable day."

I set down the box of beef and broccoli I'm holding. "What do you say that for our second date, we do something every bit as memorable?"

She swallows the bite she's eating a little too quickly and nearly chokes. "Second date?"

"Obviously, today was our first date."

She raises an eyebrow in challenge.

"I very distinctly remember me, looking all manly as I pulled lumber out of the bed of my truck, and you, asking me out on a date to the park. In fact, I also remember begging being involved. And," I motion at the table, "dinner."

"Well, then," Addi pauses to take a sip of her soda, "I think it's only fair for there to be begging involved when it comes to asking for a second date."

I hold up one finger and grab my soda with my other hand. I take a long drink, then clear my throat, get down on both knees on the carpet between the couch and the coffee table, and bring my hands together. "Addison Sparks, I would like to beg you to go on a date with me. Preferably one that doesn't involve the police or possible kidnapping charges."

"And no parks, frogs, snails, snakes, or insects?"

I nod. "We'll even take tadpoles out of the running. What do you say?"

Addison bites her lip, looking up at the ceiling like she's

trying to decide. All I can focus on is her lips. Then she meets my eyes and says, "If it can be a spontaneous date. Not planned in advance."

I cock my head. "Interesting request. Deal."

I stand and hold out my hand to shake on it, and when she puts her hand in mine to shake, she instead tugs, pulling herself off the couch and to a standing position just inches in front of me. She's close enough that I can feel her breath on my neck. I'm not sure I'm breathing at all.

As the sun sets, throwing brilliant colors behind the woods just out from the giant bay windows in front of us, she holds my eyes, and I study hers. I get the distinct impression that a decision is being made. I desperately hope that whatever it is, it keeps her standing this close to me.

She reaches out and places a hand on my chest, right over my heart, and my pulse races, electricity buzzing through me at her touch.

Then she slowly, nervously, carefully, like she's testing whatever decision she's made, slides her hand up to my shoulder, her fingertips barely skimming the skin at the edge of my collar, sending chills up the back of my neck. I keep my eyes on hers, trying to guess exactly what she's thinking, but when her eyes flick to my lips, I can't help my gaze falling to hers.

Her eyes lock on mine once again before she rises up on her toes and presses her lips into mine. It surprises me. But at the same time, it feels inevitable—like everything since that first moment in the grocery store has been leading up to this. Maybe from the first moment when she was ten and I was eleven, and I saw her through the gate between my grandparents' backyard and her aunt's inn's grounds.

I wrap my arms around her, placing one hand on the small of her back and the other in the middle of her upper back, reveling in how it feels to hold her as her lips move against mine. After Cara called off our wedding, I hadn't imagined ever being interested in a relationship again. But everything with Addi just feels right.

She brings her other arm up, wrapping both of them around my neck, holding me just as close as I'm holding her. My heart races, beating a rapid Coryce against my chest, my fingers tingling, my head light.

When she breaks the kiss to take a few deep breaths of air, I take a long, slow breath to ground my senses, and then I place three gentle kisses in a trail from her temple down to the spot just under her earlobe, enjoying the short, quick breath she inhales.

"Wow," I say. "I am really glad that Bex insisted on leaving us alone for dinner." And then I soak in the smile that Addi gives me in return.

CHAPTER 14

Addison

I'VE HELPED a lot of people organize their clothes. Some have big walk-in closets, some have taken over closets in other rooms in the house, and one client even turned a spare bedroom into a closet. With every person, I usually find one item that they hoard. I've helped people with massive collections of shoes, sweaters, shirts, dresses, pants, humorous t-shirts, scarves, and even a client with a huge collection of every style of socks imaginable.

But this woman's Achilles hoarding heel is bras. *Bras.* Bras are the worst item of clothing to shop for—even worse than jeans. Why would someone pick that item of clothing to over buy? Apparently, this thirty-one-year-old advertising executive never buys a shirt without buying a bra to match. She says it makes her feel secretly well-organized. Like it gives her superpowers.

As I'm putting bra after bra on four hanging organizers that each hold a dozen, my mind can think of nothing except the kiss last night. Actually, it's the only thing I've been able to focus on all morning.

Well, that, and everything leading up to it. For five hours straight, I witnessed firsthand how Ian reacted to what was often a stressful situation. And every time, he helped calm things when they got out of control, paused to help one of the kids, came up with a fun game for them, calmed me when things were crazy, or comforted me when things were hard. Over and over, I fell a little more for him, somehow forgetting any reservations I had about dating someone new.

And then, as we ate, I fell even harder. I worried it might've been because of how exhausted I was and the fact that I had fallen pretty hard into that couch, but even in the light of a new day, I feel all of the butterflies constantly in my stomach and the tingles that race up my spine at every thought of him.

I haven't exactly had the best experience when it comes to guys feeling the same way about me that I feel about them, and last night, I was afraid. All through dinner, I kept hoping that he'd give a very obvious sign that he was feeling even a bit of what I was feeling. I didn't think I'd get it, but then he asked me out.

And then I gathered up every single bit of courage I could find and convinced myself that I was brave enough to be the one to go in for our first kiss.

It's not that I never kiss guys. It's that I've probably kissed fewer than anyone else who lives at the inn. Probably fewer than most twenty-six-year-olds on the verge of twenty-seven. But I know enough to know what to expect.

And that expectation is exactly why I'm still so blown

away by Ian's kiss. I hadn't even imagined that kissing could be so incredible. Just remembering how his hands felt on my back, his breath on my cheek, the faint smell of wood he still had from working in the shop that morning, the softness of his lips against mine, those kisses by my ear, all while I'm pressed against his chest, is causing goosebumps to cover my arms all over again.

"Addison."

The voice of Jessie, my client, is insistent enough that I realize I've gotten a little too far into my own head. From where I sit on her closet floor, I look up at the woman, whose cleaning and organizing outfit of choice is a baggy pair of sweats and a t-shirt that says "The Office" on it. It's a very different look than the pantsuit and heels she wore at our first meeting. Jessie has her hand on a tote that sits on the bed, but I can't guess what she was just talking to me about.

"Yes?"

"You are somewhere else today, aren't you?" A smile spreads slowly across her face. "It's because of a guy, isn't it? All morning, you've had *I'm currently daydreaming about someone* face."

Based on how hot my ears suddenly are, I'm sure that face is covered in a deep pink blush.

Jessie sits down cross-legged on the closet floor in front of me. "Tell me about him."

I finish hanging up the bra I'm holding and let out a long, slow breath before meeting Jessie's eyes. "He's a guy I kissed last night. Which was probably a big mistake because he's my next-door neighbor."

"I guess that depends. On a scale of one to ten, how would you rate the kiss?"

I look down at the floor of the closet, smiling. "Ten. A ten so solid and far up there that I hadn't even known ten could be that high."

Jessie squeals like we're teenagers. "Then it's not a mistake, regardless of how it ends."

"Maybe. All I know is I've got to get my mind off him. Like right now. What's that tote you've got on the bed?"

Jessie reaches up and pulls it onto the floor next to us. "I was wondering if you have any ideas for how to organize my swimsuits. I went through them last night and narrowed it down to thirty."

My eyebrows shoot up. "Swimsuits are the only thing I can think of that's worse to shop for than bras. How are they what you collect? Do you have a trophy somewhere in here awarded for leveling up your shopping skill to the highest it goes? Maybe a medal, a ninja belt?"

Jessie laughs a tinkling little laugh, and I take the moment to force myself back into my actual job until this organization project is finished, and far away from that amazing kiss.

Since Jessie is an early riser, we finished her closet by noon, and as I head back to Quicksand, my brain is so jumbled from the mess of thoughts constantly swirling inside that I decide I really need to talk things out. Not with my roommates, though, because I already know what they'll say. I need my sister. So I pull over to the side of the road and send her a quick text.

> Addison: Hey, Sis! I really want to talk to you about Ian.

Her response comes quickly.

> Chloe: And I really want to listen to you talk about Ian.

> Addison: I also kind of really want you to meet him first. How would you feel if I invited him to join in on our birthday call?

> Chloe: Oh my gosh. This is huge. YES PLEASE.

> And then tomorrow, I better get a phone call where you talk about him.

> Addison: You sound too excited. DON'T EMBARRASS ME CHLOE.

> Chloe: I wouldn't dream of it.

> Addison: And Chloe, guess what?

> Chloe: You're smitten?

> Addison: Not the point. The point is, there's a good chance Ian will say yes.

Even though I just thought of it, and will be giving him almost no notice.

Just like he said yes to helping me babysit yesterday with no notice.

And even though it's not Tuesday or Saturday!

Chloe: This is dream-come-true stuff for you right now, isn't it?

Addison: It's not that I need a guy to be spontaneous all the time. Or even most of the time. I just need to know that he can be.

Chloe: I can't wait to meet him!

Addison: Chloe, I need to hear that you won't embarrass me.

Chloe: Aww! Dustin is lighting a birthday brownie for me. Gotta go! See you in 30 minutes!

I'm not sure if Dustin really is bringing her a brownie, or if it was just Chloe's way of getting out of making the promise. It doesn't help my nerves when it comes to texting Ian. Sure, we kissed, but I still don't really know how he feels about me. So I straighten my shoulders, slide the mirror on the visor open, and say out loud, "You can be brave. You were brave last night, and look what it got you." And of course, just thinking about it again makes me smile.

Before I know it, I'm typing a text message to him.

> Addison: Do you have a lunch break today?
> If so, are you free? I am having a video chat
> with my sister at 1:00, and I'd love to have
> you meet her.

I send the text then realize I probably should've included an apology. Feeling unsure, I figure I should also give him an easy way out.

> I know it's midday on a weekday and you're
> at work—she's nine hours ahead, so we
> had to plan it while she's awake. But there
> will be other times when you can meet her.

I pull the gearshift into drive, deciding I'm too nervous to wait around for an answer that might very well be no. But he responds before I can even take my foot off the brake.

> Ian: I will be there with bells on.

My heart soars somewhere around the top of my car the entire drive home. I hope I'll have a couple of minutes to get inside, set up my laptop, maybe run a brush through my hair and put on some lip gloss, but as soon as I pull into a parking spot, Ian walks over from his house. He must've either been working in his shed or come home from a job for lunch.

CHAPTER 15

Addison

I CAN'T STOP STARING at Ian as he strides toward me. He's so calm and confident without being cocky. The wind is even blowing the right amount to ruffle the slight wave in his hair. All I need is a video camera and the ability to watch it in slow motion, and I'd have my eyes glued to the screen for hours.

I shake myself as I realize I've frozen mid-step, gawking at him. I need to figure out what I should be doing other than mimicking a statue, but then Ian says, "Hi," as he nears, and my brain stops working.

"Hi," I say back, taking in those piercing eyes that are gazing at me, and I try not to imagine what it would be like if he walked right up to me, put his arms on my back, and dropped me into a dip, kissing me right in the driveway.

No drop kiss happens, but he does step up very close to me and tucks a curl behind my ear, then runs his fingertips down my neck, across my shoulder, and down my arm to my fingertips, sending thrills throughout my body and really not helping my ability to form words. I don't want to lose the ability to walk without falling, too, so I try to avoid looking into his eyes. In fact, turning and walking toward the door sounds like the safest course of action. So I do, pulling my keys out of my purse.

"I know you wanted our second date to be spontaneous, but I thought I was going to be the one doing the asking this time."

I glance at him as we walk up the porch steps. "This isn't a date."

"I don't know. You asked me over to meet your family. That sounds pretty date-ish."

I point at him with my keys before putting them into the lock. "Not my family—just my sister. It's so when we talk about you, she'll be able to picture you better."

He looks like he's trying to hold back a smile but isn't very successful at it. "Then I fully support this non-date."

I open the door to a lobby filled with balloons and a big sign that reads, *Happy Birthday, Addison!*

"It's your birthday?"

I duck my chin but glance at the beautiful man next to me. "Um, yeah."

"Why didn't you say anything?"

I walk to the check-in counter where a cupcake with a candle waits, along with a piece of paper that reads *Happy 27th!* in fancy handwriting—probably Peyton's doing—and *Remember that we're having a roommate dinner at 7:00 to celebrate!* below it.

"I don't know—it's awkward. How do you even bring

that up? After our kiss last night, was I just supposed to say, 'Oh, by the way, my birthday is tomorrow'?" I grab my laptop off the counter and start walking up the stairs, Ian at my side.

"That might not have been the most elegant way to bring it up, but it would've been effective."

"Oh, but see, my roommates were both elegant and effective. So it worked out well that they took it into their very capable hands."

He raises an eyebrow but doesn't say anything.

I'd thought about setting up my laptop in the gathering room but I don't want any of my roommates walking in during the call. That's the thing about living in an inn full of creative women who run their own businesses—the hours are strange, sometimes ridiculously long, and it wouldn't be entirely unusual for any or all of them to walk in at 1 p.m. on a Thursday.

If it was just me and Chloe on the call, I'd set up in my room. But with Ian with me, that feels much too intimate. So I lead him to the storeroom instead. It's a bedroom we could use for another roommate, but instead, it holds all my storage supplies for clients I'll meet with in the next two weeks on one side, some of Timini's sewing supplies and equipment on the other, and a bed pushed up against the wall that Timini and I both use more as a couch or a table when we're working in here.

Once my laptop boots up, I get it situated on a container I'm going to use for wrapping paper storage for a client and go into the video chat. Chloe's call comes through about three seconds later, and when her face pops up on the screen, she's nothing but exuberant smiles. I introduce Chloe and Ian to each other, and Chloe's husband, Dustin, pokes his head in to say hello before leaving us to our call.

"Happy birthday, Addison!"

"Happy birthday, Chloe!"

"Wait," Ian says. "It's both your birthdays?"

"You didn't tell him?" Chloe asks.

"She didn't even tell me it was her birthday."

I hold in a grimace, glance at Ian, and motion to the screen. "This is my inelegant way of telling you that we share a birthday." His hand is next to mine, and I have to ignore the fact that our shoulders are brushing together or I won't be able to think. "Except for the year Chloe was born and was in the hospital for my second birthday, we've spent every one of our shared birthdays together. This year it's just over video instead of in person."

"So you're two years apart in age, yet both of your birthdays are on the *exact same day*?"

We both nod.

"Wow. Your parents must've…"

I laugh when his comment trails off. "I know what you're thinking—I got there too when I was a kid. The very day I found out how babies were made, I Googled exactly how many days it took from conception to birth, did the math, and was one hundred percent confident that I discovered what day of the year we were both conceived."

"And from that year forward," Chloe says, "you couldn't convince Addi to stay home that night for anything."

"Come on. Do we have to tell him this story? It's embarrassing."

"Yes, we do, because you didn't tell him it was my birthday. So for the first couple of years after Addison's discovery, she'd call our grandparents and ask if we could sleep over. When we got a little older, we planned things with friends until curfew. I, of course, being the little sister, didn't understand what was going on."

"Because I, the big sister, was trying to shield you from the horror."

Chloe shoots me a look, then turns her focus to Ian. "All she told me was that we couldn't be home because that was the night of the year that our parents made babies, and you never knew when there would be another one. When I asked how they made babies, she just said, 'It's gross, and trust me: we don't want to be there for it.'

"She wouldn't tell me anything more. I remembered hearing from someone at school that their parents told them it was a 'special kind of hug.' So, that's what I had to go on. A gross, special kind of hug. Then, not long after, we had a barbeque with some family friends. My dad was out at the grill, my mom was stirring something on the stove, and Chloe and I were playing with their son Griffin.

"I went to tell my mom something and caught Griffin's parents in the hallway. They were hugging, and Griffin's dad's hands were cupping his mom's rear. Which, of course, was so gross. I thought, 'This is it. This is how babies are made.' So for three years—" Chloe shoots me a glare— "*three years*, I believed that was how babies were made."

Ian laughs so heartily that the sound practically bounces off the walls. "I think that might be the greatest story I've ever heard."

"Okay, for the record," I say, my ears getting hot, "I didn't know that was what she had assumed until much later."

"And you fully believed it?" Ian asks.

"Well, yeah," Chloe says, "because get this: when Griffin came to school on Monday, for show-and-tell, he announced that his mom was pregnant and he was getting a little brother."

"Well, obviously you believed it. Griffin practically handed you proof of your theory."

"See?" Chloe says, motioning to Ian, thrilled she's getting vindication all these years later for her misinterpretation of the facts.

Ian laughs, and I want to reach out and touch the smile lines at the edges of his eyes. Then he turns to me and says, "See? This is why, even if it's in-elegant, you should go for the effective way of telling someone something, instead of letting them figure it out on their own."

Chloe is grinning from ear to ear. Ian is so funny and charming and sweet, and I can barely keep my eyes off him. I can tell from how Chloe is reacting to him that she genuinely likes him and would totally support me being "smitten" with Ian. And who wouldn't? He's pretty great. It still feels so unreal that he's interested in me.

I smack him in the arm. "You just wait until that request comes back around to bite you."

His smile is big and beautiful. And then he picks up my hand, places the sweetest kiss on the back of it, and mumbles, "I look forward to it."

Embarrassing story after embarrassing story, the call

finally ends, and I thoroughly regret having given Chloe the opportunity to tell so many. I should've called Chloe to ask about inviting Ian to the video chat instead of texting her. Then I could've made her promise on a stack of Bibles not to tell stories about our childhood.

I walk Ian to the front door and open it for him. He pauses in the doorway, then turns back to face me. "Do you want to go on a date with me?"

"Those stories didn't scare you away?"

His smile is big. "Quite the opposite. So are you free right now?"

"What? No. You can't miss work today because of me. You already took the entire afternoon off yesterday to help me babysit."

"And I'll be scrambling to make up for lost time later, but it's your birthday, and we've got five hours until you need to be back for your roommate dinner." He reaches out and takes my hand, tugging me toward him. "Come on. Let's go on a spontaneous date."

Our hands are touching and his captivating blue eyes are pulling me to him like we are, once again, magnets. I'm not sure I could tell him no to a spontaneous date with this beautiful man any easier than I could walk away from a sale on office supplies.

So I nod. "Okay, a spontaneous date it is."

CHAPTER 16

Ian

I HOLD Addi's door open as she climbs into my truck. "Where are we going on this date?"

I close her door, walk around to my side, and get in. "I don't know. You wanted spontaneity, so I think we should decide as we go." I tap my lips, thinking. "It is beautiful outside. We could go for a walk through town, or maybe even go check out the viewpoint?" I hope I've said it in a way that makes my preference for the viewpoint slightly known—enough to sway her to that choice but not enough to make it feel like it wasn't hers.

"Ooh! Let's go to the viewpoint. I haven't been there since I was about eleven."

A smile spreads across my face as I pull out of the parking lot and head in the direction of the viewpoint. "You've been here, what? Eight or nine weeks? How is it that you haven't been to the viewpoint?"

"I guess I forgot about it. Do you go there often?"

I shake my head. "Mostly when I need to think or if I want to feel… centered."

The drive to the viewpoint is only a couple of minutes long, but I enjoy every moment of the drive with Addison sharing the front seat with me. I want to reach out and hold her hand, but even though we kissed last night, the action still feels big. From the corner of my eye, I see her pinky twitch toward me, like she wants to reach out but is waiting for me.

So I reach out, sliding my hand into hers, and she curls her fingers around mine immediately. The smile on my face is probably going to be stuck there for the rest of the day.

I pull into the parking area at the viewpoint. Only one other vehicle is here—the one I expected. After I open Addi's door for her, we walk to the guardrail at the edge of the parking lot and look out across the valley filled with trees. Only a few clouds dot the sky, casting giant shadows across the valley while the sun lights up parts of it in brilliant greens and gold. Quicksand River meanders through the valley, framed in the distance by the ridge of the Devil's Backbone and the brilliant white of Mount Hood. "I forgot how beautiful it is here," Addi breathes.

I step up next to her, marveling at the valley. We move to the telescopes to see everything closer, and while she looks, I glance up the road. Cory should be here any minute.

"I don't think I've ever been here on such a clear day," Addi says. "Check it out—you can see the sun glinting off the river clear out there."

As I look through the telescope, I hear the sound of wheels on gravel behind me. It's all I can do to keep looking through the telescope until I hear a woman say, "Excuse me."

I turn to see Cory and his girlfriend, Becca, each with one foot on the flat base of an electric stand-up scooter, one hand on the handlebars, and a helmet tucked under their other arm.

"We rented these scooters at the little station on Settler's Boulevard. We were about to put them in the back of our truck to return them, but they're paid for until five. Are you two interested in taking them?"

"You're okay trusting a couple of strangers to get them back in time?" I ask.

The grin on Cory's face is going to give him away. "You two look trustworthy."

I turn to Addi and raise an eyebrow. "What do you think?"

"Sounds fun!"

Perfect. Cory and Becca drive off, so I leave my truck behind, and the two of us put on the helmets and head down the road on the scooters, the wind blowing in our faces as we ride. I keep glancing over at Addi to see if she's having fun or hating it, and the look of bliss on her face tells me I've made a good choice.

When we reach the end of the road and stop at the stop sign, I say, "What do you think? Should we head toward town?"

She nods and turns right. Each time we come to a road where we have a choice of which way to turn, I glance over at her. I can mostly tell which way she's thinking about choosing before she does it, so I only make the choice when hers would've taken us away from where I'm aiming.

We're getting closer to the middle of town when I spot the small food truck up ahead. "What do you think? Should we stop in the shade by that truck so we can decide where to go next?"

Addi nods and heads toward it.

When we pull to a stop, I take off my helmet. "What did you think of the scooters?"

"This was the funnest thing I've done in so long! I think I'm going to have to get one of these for myself sometime."

I hadn't been sure if she'd like them or not, so I'm thrilled that's her reaction.

The guy at the food truck, Rohan, pokes his head out of the window. "Hey. The lunch rush is done, so I'm packing up. I have enough fresh lemonade for a couple of cups full that I'd hate to throw out. You two interested?"

"Wow, thanks," I say. "We would love some."

After Rohan gives us our drinks and we thank him profusely, we sit at the picnic table in front of the truck.

"Does this kind of luck always follow you around?" Addi asks. "Because it doesn't for me, so I figure it must be you."

I shake my head. "Not for me, either. I think it must be the two of us together."

As we finish and get back on our scooters, I cock my ear in the general direction of the high school. "Do you hear music?"

Addi cocks her head too, concentrating. "I'm not sure."

"I swear I hear it. Want to find its source?"

The grin on her face says she's up for the adventure, which doesn't surprise me. We head off on our scooters, with me mostly choosing which direction we take until we're close enough to really hear the music. Then I let Addi lead us the rest of the way to the high school. The entire band class has their chairs, music stands, and instruments set up on the lawn just outside the band room.

"Do they always practice outside?" Addi asks as we pull to a stop at the edge of the parking lot by the grass.

I shrug. "Want to stay and listen for a bit?" I motion to a woman sitting with her two little kids on a blanket, watching the practice. "Looks like it's okay to."

Addi nods, so we get close and stand with one foot on our scooters, watching. Less than a minute later, the woman comes up to us, her toddler in her arms, the preschooler standing next to her. "Can you two do me a huge favor? My husband is the band director—we came to watch them practice. But my son needs to use the restroom, and I don't want to pack up all our stuff to take him. Do you mind sitting on my blanket until I get back so the wind won't blow it away?"

"We'd be happy to," Addi says, and we sit on the blanket, legs outstretched, leaning back on our arms as the band plays a concert for two.

When they finish the song they'd been practicing when we arrived, they start playing Ed Sheeran's *Perfect*—a song I heard playing in Addi's room when I was helping Timini move in, so I figure there's a good chance she likes it. And I'm right. She snuggles in closer to me and whispers, "I love this song."

They play a variety of songs, and each time, the band

teacher says something like, "Let's do the song we've been practicing for halftime," or, "Let's do our concert number." Then, after about fifteen minutes, he says, "Let's practice the one we do for birthdays."

Addi's eyes flash to mine, a look of wonder on her face. It's beautiful, and I try to memorize her expression and everything about the way she looks at this moment.

As they play the first few notes, I murmur in her ear, "Looks like the universe wants you to have a great birthday."

She turns and murmurs back, "I think the universe is doing a pretty amazing job of it." Her breath is warm and soft against my neck, and between her words and her breath, heat spreads through my chest.

Right after the last notes of the *Happy Birthday* song, the mom and kids come around the corner, so we stand up. With my back to Addi, I mouth, "Perfect timing" to the mom and give her a thumbs up.

We meander on the scooters through streets neither of us has been on before, just talking about random things. I find out she likes baby goats, things organized alphabetically, and cheesecake, but really doesn't like her mom's meatloaf or pens that write in black ink. Her favorite way to relax is watching home organization shows, she has an irrational fear of revolving doors, and she gets the cutest dimples on her cheeks when she's thinking about something that makes her happy.

The more time I spend around Addi, the more I realize how truly good a relationship can be. For so long, I've been hurt that Cara called off our engagement and canceled our whole future together. As Addi and I ride scooters and chat, I finally realize that, although Cara could've handled things differently, she wasn't mean or malicious. Calling off the wedding had been the right thing to do. By ending things, Cara opened the possibility for me to have a life with Addi.

And imagining what a life with Addi might be like is a million times more incredible than anything I ever imagined with Cara. My whole soul fills with a forgiveness toward Cara that I hadn't realized I'd been holding back until this moment.

Just before five o'clock, we head back toward Settler's Boulevard and return the scooters to the kiosk.

"How are we going to get back to your truck now? Maybe we should've just ridden back to the viewpoint and put them back in your truck to bring them here."

Except that would mess with the next part of my plan. So, I shrug. "It's your birthday and we're together, so I'm sure the universe will have our backs on that, too. Want to go for a walk down Settler's?"

We chat more as we walk by shops and restaurants, enjoying the rare cloud-free day. As we walk past the front of a café, a man inside knocks urgently on the bay window. When we turn to look, he holds up one finger, asking us to wait, then races around the other tables in the café to the door. He opens it at about the same time we reach it, and he says, "My wife and I just finished eating, and they've cleaned up the plates. They were about to bring us dessert, but my wife just went into labor, so we have to leave. Do you two want to come in and have the dessert? It's already paid for, and I'd hate for it to go to waste."

Addi looks blown away by how this date is turning out, and I'm thrilled. We go inside, thank the couple, wish them the best with the delivery, and then sit down in their seats.

"What are the chances of this happening, especially after everything else magical today?" Addi asks, her voice filled with wonder.

I shrug, doing my best to keep the grin off my face.

The waitress comes over to our table, holding a dish with a slice of chocolate cake, two scoops of vanilla ice cream, and a candle sticking up out of the ice cream. Three other employees trail behind her. "What's your name, honey?" Addi looks confused. "What's going on?"

"The couple who were here before ordered this dessert with a side of birthday wishes, so I need your name for when we sing happy birthday."

"Okay," she says, eyeing me suspiciously as I do my best to look perfectly innocent and just as surprised as she is. "Addison."

The four employees sing their restaurant's version of *Happy Birthday*, and guests at a few other tables join in. After the waitress sets the dessert on the table and says, "I hope you have a wonderful birthday," Addi goes back to eyeing me as she picks up her fork and gets a bite of the cake. I scoop up a bite too, making sure to get some ice cream with it, while she continues to analyze me as we both chew.

"Did you set this up?"

"I'm pretty sure the couple who just left did that." I put another bite in my mouth, keeping my expression as neutral as possible.

"Ian. You still do that eyebrow thing you did as a kid

whenever you're not telling the whole truth. Confess. You knew it was my birthday before today, didn't you?"

"Yes," I say slowly, "but I didn't know until last night."

"Bex?"

I nod. "Moments after I left the inn last night, Bex knocked on my kitchen door. When I opened it, she said, 'Remember how I said I owe you for watching my sister's kids today? I'm going to start paying you back by letting you know that Addison's birthday is tomorrow, since I know she didn't tell you.'" I give Addi a look, reminding her how I feel about the fact that she didn't tell me. "Then I started making calls."

"So you knew the couple who was here before us?"

I nod. "Caden and Danielle. Caden's a buddy of mine who does the electrical work at a lot of the same sites as me."

"His wife didn't just go into labor?"

"She still has two or three weeks. I bribed them with the meal they ate before we got here if they'd set up this," I say as I point at the dessert with my fork, then I load up another bite.

As I chew, I see her working through the date in her mind, analyzing each thing. Her expressions switch between confusion and realization. "And the couple who gave us the scooters?"

"My friend Cory and his girlfriend Becca. They took them for a ride along Ridge Street and planned it so they'd be at the viewpoint by two-thirty."

She shakes her head in disbelief, but there's amazement there too. Like she's impressed. "You set up the lemonade too, didn't you?"

I nod. "I stopped by this morning on my way to a job and ordered them, then talked Rohan into playing along, which he was way more excited about doing than you'd guess."

"Don't tell me you set up the band, too."

I smile and shrug, then I take a bite of the cake. "This really is delicious. You better have some more before I accidentally eat it all."

"How?"

"The high school band? My grandma is friends with the band director's grandma. She asked if they'd practice outside, and his wife wanted to join in on the fun by getting the blanket there and ready for us."

"And you planned all of this today?"

"Nah. A lot of it happened last night."

"And you did all this for me?"

I want to reach out and smooth the disbelief from her face.

"Just so I could have the perfect 'spontaneous' date?"

"*And* so you could have a great birthday."

"Ian, I..." She trails off, pressing a knuckle below her bottom eyelashes. "I think it's the sweetest thing anyone has ever done for me."

Her words hit me like a warm wave, and I know I've made the right choice. She looks at me with those beautiful eyes rimmed in gold, and I can tell she's touched by the effort. It makes all the time and planning completely worth it.

"So, how were you going to get us back to your truck?" she asks.

In a move I couldn't have planned the timing on better, a

man bursts into the restaurant and says, "Anyone need an Uber? I was supposed to pick someone up, but they said never mind. I can take you anywhere in Quicksand that you need to go—it's already paid for."

And then, to my surprise, Addi leans across the table, grabs my collar, pulls me closer, and kisses me on the lips.

CHAPTER 17
Addison

I DON'T STEP through my front doorway—I float through it. As soon as the door closes, I lean against the wall, breathing out the biggest happy sigh of my life. All three roommates rush into the lobby.

"How has your birthday been?" Timini asks.

"Have you had a good day?" Peyton is practically bouncing.

"I thought you were only working until lunchtime," Bex says, trying and failing to look innocent. "I'm surprised to see you just getting home."

"You all need acting classes. Bex, Ian already spilled the beans about you sneaking over to tell him it's my birthday."

Timini grins. "So how was the date? I saw you two on scooters."

"It was so amazing," I breathe. "Best date of my life."

"Oh my lands, Addison! That's so wonderful!" Peyton

claps her hands together. "Isn't that so wonderful? It's what we've all been hoping for! And to have it on your birthday is just perfect."

"Come," Bex says, herding us toward the kitchen. "Talk around the table. Food's getting cold."

As soon as I step through the doorway, the oddest scents hit me. I sniff, trying to figure out what they could have possibly made for dinner, and fail. I'm not even sure if I think it smells good or not.

"My plan," Timini says, motioning to the messy kitchen, "was to make chicken scampi. I found a recipe and thought I could do it. I had the timing worked out on each part of it, too. But really, that just meant that every single part burned at exactly the same time."

"But the timing was flawless," Bex says as we all sit down at the table.

"Bex helped me clear out the smoke and get everything thrown out so we wouldn't keep smelling it. And then we— okay, mostly Bex—threw together chicken fajitas out of practically no ingredients at all."

"And I brought cake!" Peyton adds.

"This is perfect," I say. "Absolutely perfect. I started the day pretty bummed because it was going to be my first birthday without my sister. But you all made it wonderful."

"Well," Bex says, clearing her throat, "I don't think it was only us who made it wonderful."

My cheeks warm just thinking about the date. "Okay, Ian helped quite a bit, too."

"Aww, now see?" Timini says, grabbing the dish of tortillas. "I want a guy who will make me blush like that."

"Me, too," Peyton says.

Bex grabs a couple of tortillas when they come to her. "And me."

When Bex hands the dish to Peyton, Peyton says, "I don't think you can get to the blushing stage by only going on a string of first dates."

Bex picks up a cherry tomato and tosses it at her. "Or by not noticing what's right in front of your eyes."

Peyton just looks confused, which makes me laugh out loud. Someday, she might figure out that she likes her best friend. At the rate she's going, though, it might be a while.

Timini adds cheese, lettuce, and sour cream to her fajitas like she's making a work of art. "Obviously none of us have a love life worth chatting about, so tell us more about yours. We need to live a little vicariously."

"Even though you, Addison Sparks," Bex says as she piles the peppers and onions high on her fajita, "are going against our No Falling in Love pact."

"I never said I was falling in love."

Peyton laughs in a way that's very close to a snort. Her eyes go wide and her hands fly to her mouth in shock that she made the undignified sound.

"No, really," I protest. "I have just fallen in like."

"Yes," Peyton says. "Like. A very strong, can't stop daydreaming about him, thinks everything he does is perfect, notices how beautiful he is, *like*."

I nod. "Exactly. Besides, I'm not so sure this relationship will go very far, so I'm not about to let myself fall in love." *I'm not*, I say with much more convincing force in my head.

"How can you be so sure it won't go far?" Timini asks. "I

saw how you two were together today—it looked pretty magical."

"Oh, it definitely was. Like 'I'm your fairy godmother and I'm here with a wand' magical. It's the future I'm unsure about."

Bex shakes her head. "I don't get you one bit."

"I'm just..." How can I even explain? I'm just going to take Ian's advice and tell it however it comes out because inelegant is still effective. "I'm just not the girl who gets the guy. Ever. I actually had a guy say to me once, 'You're not the kind of girl that guys like to date—you're the kind they like to marry.'"

"He did not," Bex says.

"I swear to you he did."

Peyton looks around the table, eyebrows drawn together. "What does that even mean?"

I shrug as I wrap my tortilla tightly and pick it up. "I don't know. That I wear mom jeans? That I'm responsible but not fun? Who knows? But it explains why the only guy I did manage to ever keep was someone who didn't want a real relationship—just one of convenience. Kind of like how you're grateful for your microwave when you need it but you don't want to have to think about it when you're not standing there holding a plate of cold chicken casserole."

I take a bite of my fajita, which is actually pretty good despite the strange smell—apparently of burned chicken scampi—still hanging around the kitchen. Talking about Matthew doesn't hurt, which surprises and pleases me. And as long as I don't think about Ian and that I will probably lose him before long, I'm just fine.

"I think you're wrong," Timini says. "I mean, I don't know about your past, but I know you pretty well in your present. I've seen you and Ian and the looks you give each other, and I think you're wrong about your future with him."

I swallow my bite. "The point is, guys like Ian don't fall for girls like me. He's amazing! So, so, so incredibly amazing. He really could have his pick of anyone.

"If he's even ready to get serious with anyone yet. One of the reasons I planned to stay away from him was because he hadn't recovered from his broken engagement yet. And then, I don't know, life just kept pushing us together and I went and fell for him when I was trying not to."

That's the biggest part. The more time we spend together, the more I'm convinced that Ian is my happily ever after. I hope I haven't destroyed any chance I have with him—small as it might be—simply because everything between us is happening before he's ready.

I point at each of my roommates and make my words come out in a jovial tone. "So when things go wrong and I'm a blubbering mess because I let my heart get in danger, just know that I'm coming to the three people who tried to talk me into it in the first place."

"And we'll be here for you," Bex says. "We'll wrap our arms around you and tell you that you're pretty and that everything's going to be okay."

"And we'll feed you cake!" Peyton says, getting out of her seat and grabbing the layered cake from the counter behind her.

"So what I'm hearing is," I say, "that I can fall as fully for Ian as I'd like because when I fall, I have a soft spot to land."

"Exactly that," Timini says.

I take another bite and think about how easy it'd be to do exactly that. Or maybe I don't need to fall fully for him. Maybe I'm already there.

CHAPTER 18

Ian

I PULL INTO MY DRIVEWAY, turn off my truck's headlights, and get out. I never want to be the one holding any part of construction up at a site, so I stayed at the Koermer house as long as it took to finish my part, even though it meant working so late. I drag myself into the house through the kitchen door and kick off my boots.

"Grandma?"

"In my office, sweetie!"

I open the fridge and find the lasagna Grandma texted me about. I'm so hungry I could probably eat everything left in the pan, but I cut a large piece, put it on a plate, and stick it in the microwave. As it warms, I head to find her.

The sound of voices meets me as I turn the corner into the hallway, and when I enter her office, I'm rewarded with smiles from my two favorite people. Addi and Grandma are sitting across the desk from each other, going through piles of papers. After such an incredibly long day, I can't believe how great it feels to come home and see Addi's face smiling at me.

"Hi, sweetie. Did you see the lasagna?"

I nod. "It's in the microwave. Addi, have you eaten?"

She smiles as I pull her to her feet and wrap my arms around her waist. "I ate with your grandma before we got started."

I glance at Grandma, and then at the recycle bin next to her. "Are you sure you want to throw that paper on top away?"

As Grandma turns to look at the paper she tossed, I pull Addi close and kiss her, savoring the warm softness of her lips. I nudge the curls away from her ear and whisper, "It's so good to see you."

She lets out a breathy giggle as my words tickle her ear, then snuggles in a little closer, even though I'm covered in sawdust. I leave a few kisses on her neck while I'm there.

"Why would I need to keep a receipt from having our lawn aerated eight years ago? Oh! You were just trying to get me to look away. You know, I can leave the room if you want privacy."

I laugh and let my arms fall from Addi's waist so she can sit back down. "No need, Grandma. I'm going to go eat some of your lasagna."

I apparently can't stand being in the same house as Addi and not being in the same room as her, so I bring my food into the office and eat while the three of us chat. When I'm finished, I announce I'm going to take a shower and don't miss the blush that crosses Addi's cheeks. That's now officially my favorite color.

"We're working on the closet next," Addi says, "and there are a couple of boxes in there with your name on them."

"There are?" My brow furrows. I vaguely remember a few boxes I didn't unpack when I moved in after Grandpa died. I haven't thought about them since that first week.

"Yep," Grandma says, "and if you don't go through them and get your stuff organized, Addison and I are going to."

There's a teasing gleam in her eyes, but that doesn't mean she's not being serious. "Wait, really?"

She nods. "So you might want to get to them."

I look toward my room and then back at Addi and Grandma, holding out my hands like I'm trying to pause them. "Just—just leave them there. I'll take a quick shower and come right back."

I race into my room, shut the door, then go into my bathroom and shut that door, too. Hopefully, I'm quick enough. I drop the shampoo once and hit my elbow into the shower wall twice, fully aware the office is on the other side of the wall. Probably ten minutes later, I'm back in the room, wearing a clean T-shirt and jeans. If it were just Grandma and me working, I'd probably be in gym shorts, but with Addi here, I still want to look good.

They both smile as I walk in, and it's obvious they've been talking about me. I hope it's good. The closet has quite a few boxes, so I start pulling them out and organizing them based on what's written on them. I find three labeled with my name. I don't remember what's in them, but I want to be the first to look.

As I go through the first box, I remember why I didn't

already unpack these. They're full of stuff that's fun and memorable but not things I need. I'm not even sure what to do with it all. I pull out some artwork from elementary school and chuckle. Maybe I should've taken Grandma's offer to go through it with Addi.

Still, it's kind of cool to relive all the memories while chatting with Addi and my Grandma. I start making a pile of things that could go into a scrapbook, a pile of objects I want to keep but don't want sitting out, and a pile of things I want to put where I can see them—a pile that currently holds two items.

I pull the third box toward me after finishing the second. As soon as I cut the packing tape, I remember exactly what it contains. It started out as a box filled with random things that I'd only halfway unpacked when I moved here. For a long time, it sat on my closet floor with the flaps open, so I'd started tossing in mementos from when Cara and I were dating and engaged—wristbands from concerts, playbills, museum fliers, and even a restaurant receipt from our first date. When Cara ended things, the box became too much to face. I sealed it up and put it on the floor of the office until I could decide what to do with it. Grandma must've moved it to the closet.

Cara broke up with me two and a half months ago. It's been long enough that I can handle dealing with this stuff now. I start tossing mementos into the "throw away" box, getting rid of quite a few things, until I come across our wedding invitation. It sits on top of everything that's still in the box, staring at me. We'd already sent them out before Cara called the wedding off. In fact, the RSVPs had come back, the seating chart was done, and presents had started arriving.

I glance at Addi. She's going through a box with my grandma, and I'm grateful she's not witnessing any expressions on my face. Especially because all the questions I'd asked myself when Cara ended things come rushing back. Was I just not good enough? Or was I so oblivious that I hadn't seen our issues? That night, Cara had said to me, "When you asked me to marry you, I thought I wanted to spend the rest of my life with you. Now I know I don't. Not because of any one specific thing—it was just...a little of everything, I guess."

I wish it had been something specific. Then I'd know. But since it wasn't, I have to assume it was everything. I was happy enough in our relationship, and at the time, I thought that was adequate. It hadn't dawned on me that Cara's expectations, dreams, and vision for our future couldn't be realized.

Sometimes I worry that I must not be husband material. Other times, I force those doubts away and remind myself that it's not true. But when I do, the nagging thought creeps in: maybe Cara and I just weren't a good match. If that was the case, then I'd failed to see it. And that's an issue all on its own.

Cara and I worked together to undo all the wedding preparations—to cancel everything, return everything we bought for the reception, send back the gifts, and get out of the contract for the apartment we were days away from moving into. It was mentally tough and so draining. If my judgment had been solid, I would've realized our issues before it got that far.

I can't handle dealing with anything else in this box related to the wedding that never happened. I shift a big stack of memorabilia and cards to see if there's anything else underneath it that I need to go through and spot the edge of a rock. I reach in and pull out the flat stone, smiling.

The scene Addi painted is exactly as I remember it. I run my finger across the trees by the shore and the way the river curves outward in our favorite spot, making the water calmer and perfect for jumping in. Not that it was deep—most of the time, it barely reached our knees. Even though little Ian and little Addi are only about an inch high in the painting, she still managed to capture the big smiles on our faces as we held hands and jumped in.

"You really did keep it," Addi breathes.

I glance up to see her looking at the stone and smile. "Of course, I did."

Then a stabbing pain hits me. What if things go wrong with Addi? Can I handle the pain of going through with her what I went through with Cara? With Addi, I'm happy. More than happy—I'm thrilled. I am so much happier now than I was at any point in my relationship with Cara. If things go wrong with Addi and me, I'll have so much further to fall.

I put the stone back into the box and stand. "Listen, I've got to go. I'm sorry to run out on you two, but I have to…" What? I don't even know, so I can't finish my sentence. I just need to go somewhere and think.

After giving Addi a quick kiss on the forehead, I grab my keys and shoes and head out to my truck for a long drive.

CHAPTER 19

Addison

That's how Chloe answers the phone when I call her on my way to the grocery store on Saturday morning. "What if you won't like the news?"

"No, Addison! *No bad news.* There can't be bad news. You two are too adorable together. What happened?"

"I don't know. Maybe nothing. Maybe something."

"Oh. That explains everything."

"It does?" Chloe has so much more experience with dating and guys and understanding what's going on.

"No, that was sarcasm. Don't they have sarcasm in Oregon? Explain."

"You know how I was worried about Ian being a rebound guy for me? Well, I realized that rebounding for me wasn't about getting past feelings for my ex, because Matthew and I never had very strong feelings for each other.

What I most miss about our relationship is the security of knowing right where I stood with him."

"Please don't tell me you're thinking of going back to Matthew."

"No. Not at all. I want a relationship where the amount of love we feel for each other is at a ten. With Matthew, it never got over a three. But it was a solid three, and I really miss that it was so solid.

"When I'm with Ian, he is so sweet, and it feels like we are connecting so well, and I just *know* he really likes me. And then other times, we just…don't, and it leaves me feeling unsure about everything. Like last night. I was helping his grandma in her office and he came home from work. You should've seen his face, Chloe. It completely lit up when he saw me. Like I am his entire world. I wish I had a video of it so I could just watch it over and over."

Chloe happy sighs.

"And then we were all working on organizing the office and just chatting about random things, and he got really quiet. I looked over to see what was up, and he was holding the stone I painted for him. Remember that?"

"Oh, I remember. I swear you talked about it for a year straight."

"There was just something different about him while he was holding it. Heavy. Sad. Anxious. Regretful. I don't know —it's hard to explain. Then he just got up, said goodbye, and left."

"Huh." The line goes quiet for a few moments, and then Chloe asks, "Did his grandma say anything?"

I pull into a parking spot and turn off my car, then pick

up my phone when Bluetooth switches it over from the car's speakers. "She did. She said that maybe it wasn't the rock that made him all morose—maybe it was what was under the rock. So I looked. It was a wedding invitation. *His* wedding invitation."

"Get out."

I very nearly open my door at my sister's command, then roll my eyes at myself and stay put. I'm the older sister, after all.

"He didn't get married, though, right?"

"No. I knew his last relationship had been serious. He told me he'd thought it would end in marriage. I just didn't know he thought it would end in marriage because they'd actually planned the wedding. Shirley said their wedding was supposed to happen the same weekend I moved here." I let out a deep breath. "Remember all the research I did to make sure that Ian wouldn't be a rebound guy?"

"Yeah."

"I think I probably worried about that more than I needed to. What I should've been worrying about was becoming the rebound girl."

"Oh."

"So what do I do? The same thing I've been doing? Back off and give him space? Buy myself a spinning wheel and a bunch of wool in preparation for a life of solitude?"

"Communication is the number one thing. Go out with him again soon and bring it up."

"I can do that." I pause for a moment. "Thanks, Chloe, for dating a million guys before finding Dustin so you can answer my questions. Even if half a million of them were ones I had hoped would ask me out."

"What are sisters for?"

After hanging up the phone, I send a text to Ian, not allowing myself to stop and overanalyze before I do.

> Addison: Are you free tonight?

It takes long enough for his response to come in that I almost grab my list and head into the grocery store. Finally, though, I get a text.

> Ian: I'm not. I have to install all the cabinets in a home today, and it's huge. They'll be ready for me to start at noon, and I won't be finished until late.

I almost reply with a frowny-faced emoji and prepare to spend more of the weekend feeling unsettled, but then I decide that I'm not going to quit so easily.

> Addison: You still have to eat, right? How about I bring dinner to the site? And then I can help. With a little direction, of course.

> Ian: But what if you came and all I wanted to do was kiss you? I'd never finish installing the cabinets.

I keep re-reading the text, my heart doing a little jump every single time.

Addison: Then we'll have to turn it into a game. We install one cabinet, we get one kiss.

Ian: I like it when you're in charge of the games.

I smile, grab my list, and get out of the car. I can make exactly two dishes well, and one of them is chicken piccata. I already have the list of things to buy because I'm making it for my roommate dinner turn later this week, so I'll just get double.

———

I pull up to the house Ian texted me the address for. It's a newer neighborhood with three houses under construction next to each other, and he wasn't kidding when he said it's huge.

Ian must sense me pulling up because he comes out quickly enough to reach me before I even get the passenger door open. He gives me a big smile and a kiss, then says, "That one didn't count—the game hasn't started yet."

But to my lips, which are still tingling from feeling his, it definitely counts.

"It isn't takeout—you cooked dinner? For me?" He picks up the dish with the hot pad, then he lifts the foil and breathes in deeply, a look of bliss spreading across his face.

"Now don't get all excited. This and enchiladas are the extent of what I can cook."

I grab the basket and a blanket and follow Ian into the house. A couple of other guys are working on different things in the house, but Ian shoos them away when their noses bring them straight to the food, and he leads me into what I assume will be a guest bedroom. The carpet hasn't been laid yet, so I spread the blanket on the plywood floor. Ian puts the chicken dish I've paired with pasta on the blanket, and I pull dishes, rolls, and a green salad from the basket and place them on the blanket, too.

Ian seems to love the food and gives me compliment after compliment. Enough that I don't even want to bring up his engagement, but I know that if I don't plow ahead with my questions, I might get cold feet.

"So, you were engaged and nearly married, huh?" Wow. When I thought through this part of the night in my head, it came out so much less blunt.

Ian ducks his chin and rubs the back of his neck. "Um, yeah. I should've told you already. It was just…"

"Awkward?"

"Yeah. I meant to tell you when we had our catch-up coffee date, but before I got a chance, I was carrying you in my arms. It seemed weird to say, 'Oh, and by the way, I was engaged, but my fiancée broke it off right before the wedding.'"

"That might not have been the most elegant way to bring it up, but it would've been effective." I smile because I'm pretty sure I quoted his words pretty close to exactly.

Ian's laugh is loud and booming, bouncing off the smooth surfaces of the empty room. He scratches his cheek. "In all fairness, you did warn me that I might not like it when my request came back around to bite me, so I shouldn't be surprised."

I chuckle. But I need more info, so I prod. "And? Tell me about it."

He starts by sharing the parts that Shirley already told me. Then he tells a little about their relationship. It doesn't sound like it was bad, but it doesn't sound like it was great, either. It's a little like my relationship with Matthew, where we weren't in each other's lives enough in all the important ways.

But my relationship with Matthew had been practically unmoving for years, so it wasn't a big deal to hop off that stalled train. Ian's relationship with Cara had plowed ahead like a freight train, so when she pulled the brakes, it jumped the tracks and injured everyone. It sounds like it was awful. And the way Ian becomes more sullen and weighed down as he tells the story confirms its awfulness.

"Wow. I really brought down the mood of the room, didn't I?"

"Luckily," I say, "I brought apple cobbler. It's guaranteed to bring it back up seven notches."

"You made apple cobbler?"

I hold the container back as he grabs for it. "No, I *bought* it. I can make two things, remember? Getting your expectations higher isn't allowed."

He's still leaning forward from trying to grab the cobbler, his face inches from mine, so I kiss him. He smiles into the kiss and says, "This one doesn't count, either."

I *really* want things with us to work out. I can already picture the marital bliss—waking up next to him, kissing him as he comes home all covered in sawdust, joining forces to accomplish his goal of opening a cabinet shop and mine of opening an organizational design business and finding all the ways we'll work together. Then finding all the ways we'll work together to raise happy little children that are running around with Ian's dark, wavy hair.

We clean up dinner and start working on the cabinets. Ian and an assistant—a kid who used to be a Junior Woodworker, apparently—have hung all the upper cabinets before I got here, which is good, because those sound more difficult, and I don't have a clue what I'm doing.

If I'd ended our date right after we ate, I probably would've walked away feeling relatively confident about our relationship. As the night goes on, though, I'm less and less confident. There are times when we laugh as we work and he very enthusiastically kisses me after each cabinet is finished. At other times, he seems to be thinking too much, and it's as if he's avoiding me as much as one can while working together to maneuver a cabinet into a tight space. My attempts to find out how he's feeling fail.

It's obvious that something is wrong—he seems to be trying to hide his emotions but not managing to. We finish with the kitchen, two of the bathrooms, and one of the washrooms when I say, "You seem to be doing a lot of thinking tonight."

"I'm sorry I've been so distracted." He wraps his arm around my waist and pulls me in close. I put my arms around his neck and soak in how right it feels to be so near him. Everything about this is right. He leans in close to my ear, his breath tickling my neck. "Coming here tonight to help me was an incredible thing to do. Thank you."

My mouth is right by his ear, too, so I breathe, "You forgot to mention dinner."

I feel his smile right next to my ear, and he pulls back enough to meet my eyes. "So was bringing me a delicious meal. And giving me kisses like they were fuel to keep going."

I drop my hands to his chest. "So what you're saying is, I saved you twice today." It's what he said to me after he helped me with Bex's nieces and nephews and fed me dinner.

He chuckles and smiles that amused smile that first pulled me in at Gateway Groceries so many weeks ago. He drops one hand to my hip and brushes a curl away from my cheek with the other. "In the who-saves-whom category, it looks like we're tied. It's anyone's guess who's going to be getting that Medal of Honor in the mail."

When we finish, he picks up the picnic basket and blanket and carries them out to my car, walking hand-in-hand with me. Which is good, because he turns the power of those beautiful blue eyes on me, and my knees are suddenly too weak for me to make it on my own.

At my car, he puts the blanket and basket inside, cupping his hand so gently at the back of my head, and gives me the sweetest kiss ever. I practically melt into a puddle right by my car. The kiss alone tells me that maybe everything will work out between us just fine.

CHAPTER 20

Addison

I'M SO glad you've been able to help me today," Peyton says as I chop the last piece of cooked chicken in the tray.

"I'm glad I had the day off—it's been fun!" I never thought that spending the day cooking could actually be fun. It's a nice change of pace from my usual. It feels good to just mindlessly chop food. And Peyton has been so grateful.

"It really has." Peyton smiles her perfect smile, her hair looking pretty even while she spends the day in the kitchen. Then she removes the empty tray and puts a full one in its spot.

"More chicken?"

"This is why I'm a personal chef and not a caterer. With catering, there's so much monotony. Seriously, thank you, Addison. It's a client I cook for all the time who's having a big luncheon, but still. I don't know what I was thinking when I took this job. I couldn't do it without you."

I get lost in the rhythm of my chopping while Peyton

mixes the rest of the ingredients for the chicken salad in a giant bowl.

"How are things going with Ian?" she asks.

`I shrug. "I don't know. And I hate not knowing. All I do know is that he's everything I ever wanted but hadn't known yet. I've fallen pretty hard for him."

Peyton smiles dreamily.

"But let's talk about something else. I've already analyzed everything more than an IRS agent analyzes a suspicious tax claim, and I've got brain exhaustion from it."

Peyton's phone dings, so she washes her hands, goes to where it rests on the counter, and touches the screen. Then she smiles at it—the kind of smile I've only seen her use with one person.

"Is that a text from Max?"

She nods. "He's a funny friend."

I shake my head, wondering if she'll ever refer to him as something other than a friend.

Timini finally comes back into the room, hugging a kid-sized dress form and taking small steps so her legs don't bang into it too much as she walks. She sets it down with a huge exhale and starts adjusting its size.

"Okay, let's switch to a new subject, then," Peyton says, pulling another tray of croissants out of the oven. "How's work?"

"I kind of imagined that most of my days would be spent blissfully organizing people's homes. There is so much more to running a business that I'm learning as I go. I'm a little stressed by how many blank spots I have in my schedule coming up since that's what's paying the bills."

The truth is, I'm a lot stressed out by it. I'm not great at marketing or advertising because I didn't have to deal with that side of the business back when I worked for a company in Amarillo instead of owning a business myself. It all comes so naturally to Chloe, and it makes me wish we lived close again. With her help, I'd have my schedule filled for sure.

"I think you should just not worry about it," Timini says. "Clients will come in when they come in. Stressing about it won't change anything."

Bex drags herself into the room, wearing baggy sweats and a baggy t-shirt, her hair pulled into a messy bun, no makeup on, and flops into a chair at the table. "Guys, I'm sick. And I have episodes to film. Make me better. Please? I'm begging here."

"I'm pretty sure there's a sticky note somewhere that says it's against the rules to be sick," Timini says without even cracking a smile as she puts a half-finished bodice on the form. Me? I have to hold in a laugh.

"Get your germs away from the food!" Peyton screeches, making shooing motions. "Go sit on one of those tables."

Bex just looks at the other tables like she doesn't have the energy to get up and move. "Can't. They're too messy."

"Really, they are," I say. "Can we get a little more organized everywhere?" I don't mean to direct the comment at Timini, but she's definitely the one contributing the bulk of the chaos at the inn.

"If things are too organized," Timini says, her voice calm as she adjusts the mannequin, "then creativity flies right out the window. The same goes with rules." She shoots a glare at Bex.

"While we're discussing issues," Peyton says as she adds the chopped chicken to her mixture, "can we talk about adjusting the temperature? It's always freezing in here!"

"Are you kidding?" Bex says, looking like Peyton's comment gives her some life back. "It's always a furnace in here. Especially when you cook."

Peyton looks to Timini and me for support, but I don't say anything—I think the temperature is fine. "Okay, then, maybe we can talk about keeping the volume down a bit while we're all trying to work."

Bex sits up straighter. "Is this referring to when my sisters and their kids come over? Because loud is how you know they enjoy being around each other."

"Maybe we just need to change things up a bit," Timini says, glancing around. "Rearrange the rooms down here. Maybe all we need is an infusion of change to refresh everyone."

"No!" Peyton begs. "Change doesn't rejuvenate. It stresses people out."

This whole conversation is stressing me out. Normally, I love it when we're all together, whether we're working out issues or not. My parents were never around much, and Chloe and I didn't always have the same schedules, so I felt like I never really had much of a family growing up. All my roommates in a room together make this place feel like home.

But my nerves are too frayed from my worries about Ian and work. I duck out of the room and take a few deep, calming breaths once I get to the lobby, kind of missing the teeny apartment that I had all to myself back in Amarillo.

I stop breathing and cock my ear when I hear gurgling and popping sounds, almost like knocking. Then there's a loud hissing. I've heard the knocking before, but never the hissing, never this loud, and never when I could tell where the sounds are coming from. Walking carefully so I can hear the noise as I go, I head down the hall toward the back door and stop right in front of the utility closet. Yep, the hissing is definitely coming from in there.

More than a little wary, I reach for the doorknob just as a gush of hot water soaks my shoes. I fling the door open and see water pouring from a valve about two-thirds of the way up on the water heater. Water is gushing out, filling the little room and spilling out into more and more of the hallway.

I must've screamed because all three of my roommates are suddenly by me, frozen in shock, gasping at what they're seeing.

"We need something to catch the water!" I say as I race into the bathroom just down the hall and dump the hand towels out of the decorative bowl on the tank of the toilet. Then I run back to the water heater. Bex, Peyton, and Timini come running up the hallway, their footsteps splashing in the water, carrying bowls from the kitchen.

Bowl after bowl, one of us catches the water until the container is full, and then the next person catches the water while the first one runs it to the bathroom sink.

Finally, I shake my head. "We aren't getting to the end of it. More water must be filling it still." There's a hose connected to the top of it, so I search for some kind of valve to turn it off but can't see anything.

"We need to shut off power to it, too," Bex says,

crowding into the small room, searching for the power while I search for the water valve and Peyton holds a bowl, with the water all around us and everything going wrong.

The power is easier to find than the valve, but we eventually manage to shut both off and dump the last of the water into the sink. Even with all our efforts, the long hallway and the lobby are covered in water.

The adrenaline of stopping the water took all the energy Bex had, so she heads upstairs to bemoan her sickness alone. Timini, Peyton, and I scoop the water off the tile floor with dustpans. Eventually, we get the water amount down enough that we just have to use towels, wringing them into a bucket constantly.

When we finally finish, Timini and Peyton head upstairs to their rooms to put on dry clothes, but I just stay downstairs. Exhausted and dreading how much a new water heater is going to cost—not to mention what a pain it will be to shower and wash dishes until it's replaced—I sit down on the second stair and let my head fall into my hands, giving into the despair.

My phone, which I forgot was in my pocket, rings. I really hope it's a miracle worker calling to solve all of my problems. "Hello?"

"Hi, Addison."

It takes me a minute to place the voice. "Matthew?" I pull the phone away from my ear long enough to look at the number to verify. It hadn't occurred to me that by deleting him from my contacts, I wouldn't know it was him if he called. Sure enough, though, it's the 806 area code. I wonder if whoever wrote that website article thought about the perils of accidentally answering a call from your ex simply because you deleted his contact information.

"It's good to hear your voice. I just wanted to see how you're doing."

I sigh. "Today isn't really the best time to ask that question. How are you?"

"Good. What's happening today that's got you down?"

I shrug, even though he can't see me. I know he's only asking because it's the thing to do—Matthew has never really been interested in day-to-day details—but I tell him because he's asking and I apparently need to get it out.

"Let's just say I'm having second thoughts about my job, I'm unsure about a lot of things, actually, and right now, a teeny apartment with a landlord who swoops in to fix any problem sounds heavenly. Oh, it's rained for twelve hours straight, and I'm talking the gloomy kind of rain, and I miss the sun. You know, the kinds of things that make you question whether moving somewhere new was a mistake."

"Well, I did see a 'now leasing' sign in front of your old apartment building."

I laugh. It's obvious he's trying to lift my spirits, and it actually works. Partly because it makes me think—just for a second—about moving back to Amarillo, which helps me to realize that, awful day or not, I really don't want to. I want to be here.

"Thank you, Matthew. I guess I needed that. What's new with you? Are you dating anyone?"

He chuckles. "Actually, yeah. My Tuesdays and Saturdays got a little lonely."

"That's great news, Matthew. Everything's going well?"

"It really is."

Thinking back to how stagnant our relationship was makes me wonder how I ever thought we should stay together for as long as we did. But it surprises me how happy I am for him that he's found someone new. It's a little reminder that there's someone for everyone.

"So, listen," he says. "I was actually calling because I'm flying to Portland tomorrow for business. I still have a box of your things, and I was wondering if I could drop it by."

"Oh, sure. Yeah, that'd be great. I'll text you my address."

"And I'll let you get back to your crisis and re-evaluation of your life choices."

I chuckle, and Matthew does, too. "You sound good, Matthew. I'm glad."

"You do, too. I'll drop that by tomorrow night."

After hanging up and texting him my address, I slide my phone back into my pocket. Who says communicating with your ex is a bad idea? Talking to Matthew and finding out he's doing well and has moved on feels like closure. Like it marks the end of my rebound period. Like that part of my life is done and wrapped up all clean and neat with a bow on top.

Now I just need to figure out how to deal with the mess that my current life is.

CHAPTER 21

Ian

I GLANCE at the clock on the wall of my shop. The parents of my Junior Woodworkers are going to start showing up any minute, and we still haven't finished cleaning up. We spent most of the hour sanding their stepstools, and the kids managed to get covered from head to toe in sawdust. Probably because instead of being one hundred percent focused on them like I need to be, my mind keeps wandering to Addi. With as dusty as the kids are, their parents aren't going to want them to get in their vehicles.

Luckily, I turned on the air compressor before they arrived, so it's ready to go. "Okay, woodworkers—put your project in your cubby, get your safety goggles and dust mask on, and then come line up just outside the door."

Nothing gets them to clean up more quickly than needing to be blown off with the air hose. The first kid races out of the shop and waves at his mom, who's already waiting at the edge of the grass. I squeeze the trigger on the nozzle and blow the pressurized air on the kid as he turns in a circle, sawdust scattering to the wind. Then he leans forward so I can blow the dust out of his hair, then holds out one foot at a time so I can get his shoes.

He pulls off his dust mask and goggles and wipes away the last of the dust behind them. He turns to his mom, holding his arms straight out, a big grin on his face. "How do I look?" Leaving with hair that looks like he's been in a tornado seems to be his favorite part of the week. He says goodbye, I thank his mom, and then I start blowing the dust from the next Junior Woodworker in line.

By the time I get to the last kid, half the group has already left with their parents, and the rest are chasing each other around my backyard. Jella, one of the most talkative kids and the one with the longest hair, is last. As I blow the sawdust off her while she turns in a circle, she says, "It took my mom thirty-two minutes to brush all the snarls out of my hair after last time."

I immediately turn off the air. "I'm glad you told me before I used this on your hair then."

"No, do it! Make it as crazy as you can. I'm trying to set a new record."

I glance at the driveway, hoping her mom or grandma is there to tell me if they'd rather I skipped this part, but I don't see either of them. "How about we work on setting a record in the opposite direction? We'll try to get all the sawdust out and only need five minutes of brushing."

Jella shrugs, so I carefully blow air from the top of her head, keeping it directed straight down. But at the last second, too quickly for me to stop her, Jella shakes her head wildly, making the air blow her hair into a crazy mess anyway.

I turn off the air hose, and Jella, grinning at her messy hair, says, "You know that girl Cara who you were going to marry—the one who was sometimes waiting for you after Junior Woodworkers? I saw her."

"Yeah?" I start coiling the air hose.

Jella nods. "At Cascade Mini Golf. She was with some guy, and they were all loving on each other and kissing pretty much the whole time. I just wanted to march right up to her with my hands on my hips like this and say, 'You shouldn't be here as a pair like you don't even care. You should be home crying for a month straight because of how mean you were to Ian!' And I would've done it, too, but my grandma and mom told me I couldn't."

I can't help glancing across the hedgerow to Addi's home. "As much as I appreciate you looking out for me, Jella, it's okay that Cara is dating someone else. We aren't together anymore."

"That's what my mom said. But it just doesn't seem right that she's so happy." Jella glances at the other kids. "Oh— Priya is having trouble catching Ajay. I better go help her." And then she runs off to join the kids racing around my backyard, squealing and laughing.

More parents arrive to collect their kids, so I herd the remaining handful to the front yard. Jella's mom is the last to arrive, and I apologize about the state of her hair while Jella demands that her mom take a picture of the masterpiece.

As soon as they finally drive away, I pull out my phone and open Cara's social media, needing to see who this new guy is that Jella saw her with. Sure enough, there are several pictures of a smiling Cara with a man's arm—Dylan Brady, the tag says—wrapped around her.

A rush of an emotion I can't quite name floods me. "Jealousy" is the only word that comes to mind, but it's not quite right. I'm not jealous of Dylan. I don't want to be the one with my arm around Cara. I'm actually happy she's found someone.

So what is it, then?

I glance at Hidden Inn. I want Addi to be happy and fully in love, too. I want her to be happy and fully in love with *me*. I want to be the one who brings a smile to her face whenever I see her just like she brings a smile to mine. I want the best of everything for her.

Then I realize that the emotion hitting me feels like jealousy because I'm jealous of *Cara*. In the few pictures she posted, she looks like she's moved on just fine and has no worries about whether her new relationship could end and exactly how much it will crush her if it does.

Yet I'm having worries about mine.

I love every single second I spend with Addi and want her in my life more and more. Right now, I want to walk over to the inn, wrap my arms around her, kiss her senseless, and then hear about how things went with today's client and what her future plans are. I want her in my arms as we talk for hours.

Yet I'm still worried that she will see in me whatever Cara saw that caused her to cancel our wedding. I close out of the app and shove my phone back into my pocket. This is making me crazy and not helping at all. To help distract myself, I walk to the mailbox and grab today's mail.

Before I even look down at the mail, movement at Hidden Inn catches my eye, and I glance over. A car just pulled into the circular drive in the front, and a man gets out. He's pretty good-looking, and I assume he's here for Bex. She seems to date a lot, and it usually isn't the same person.

I walk my fingers along the top of the envelopes, glancing at what came as I head back toward my house. Then I glance over again and see Addi answer the door, not Bex. I can't see the guy's face, but I can see Addi's, and it's all recognition and smiles. The man hands her some kind of gift box, they hug, and he kisses her cheek. Then she invites him inside.

The only explanation I can think of is that it must be her ex from Amarillo. But here in Quicksand? Why? And why does she look so happy to see him?

———

As I clean up from work and eat dinner, my mind goes in circles, the tension weighing down my shoulders. Before Addi came back to Quicksand, my doubts and fears were probably in the high range. I was having a pretty rough time.

Then Addi moved in. And I got to know her as an adult. And then I really started to fall for her. Somewhere along the way, the unease and uncertainty just kind of floated away, like they didn't even exist. When I do consciously think about it, it isn't enough to cause any kind of action on my part. I've been too busy falling completely for Addi to pay it any attention.

Over the past week, though, my fears have kicked back into high gear. Especially since I've fallen for Addi so much more deeply than I ever fell for Cara. I thought I was ready to fully open my heart to her, but all these fears are making me less sure.

I wander around my house, hoping for peace or direction, but all I get when I wander into the kitchen is the little green-and-yellow origami frog my grandma folded and left on the table with a note in its mouth reminding me that she's gone to the Paperworks Folding Fest conference and won't be home until late.

I glance out the window—there's probably a good thirty minutes before it gets dark. Since wandering around my house aimlessly isn't helping, maybe I should go mow the inn's backyard. The noise and the work might get my mind off things. I put on my work gloves and head out to the gate in the hedgerow that leads to Addi's yard.

I've only made it five feet onto her lawn when she walks out the back door, a bag of trash in her hand. Our eyes meet, and she gives me a small smile, tosses the garbage into the can, and then walks toward me.

She glances at my gloves. "A little late for mowing, isn't it?"

I shrug. "It's been one of those days."

"Yeah, it has." She leans against the metal archway that holds the fence between our yards, looking exhausted or sad or upset—I'm not sure which.

I immediately leave the mower behind, stepping closer to

her. "Is everything okay?" I want to reach out and comfort her, to wrap her up in my arms. But the worry weighing so heavily on my shoulders stops me. Instead, I lean against the other side of the archway, facing her.

Addi rubs her fingers on her temples before dropping them to her sides. "Today and yesterday have just been the kind of days that make me question every decision I've made in the past couple of months."

My heart seems to suddenly weigh more, sinking down in my chest. Is that why her ex stopped by? Because she's rethinking her decision to break up with him? I'm already dreading the answer, but I still ask, "Like what?"

She looks up at the darkening sky. "Choosing to start my own business instead of getting another corporate job, leaving Amarillo, moving across the country, living at the inn instead of selling it—pretty much everything."

Her eyes search mine, and I try to guess what it is she's looking for, but alarm bells are going off too loudly in my head at the words "pretty much everything." She's unsure about every single thing that brought her here—that brought her into my life. I swallow down the lump in my throat. "Does that include your decision to date me, too?"

She studies my eyes, biting her lip. "Sometimes."

My mind keeps circling back to every negative thought I had about myself when Cara first broke things off with me. Is that the direction things are heading with Addi? I don't know if I'm strong enough for that.

But if we wait longer and I fall even more in love with her, I definitely won't be strong enough if things end.

"Listen, Addi. I…" I look at the ground, releasing a long

breath before I meet her eyes again. "I can't do this anymore." I can't believe the words actually come out of my mouth.

Addi stands up straight, her eyebrows creasing together. "This? As in *us*? You want to break up?"

No. I don't want to break up at all. I want to hear why she's questioning her job and her move and see if I can help, and I want to hold her and comfort her if I can't. I want us to cheer each other on as we reach for our dreams. I want to marry her and have a bunch of kids with her that are hopefully less wild than Bex's nieces and nephews. Or more wild. I'd take that, too, if Addi and I could do it together. I want to be with her always.

But if Addi and I get to the same point Cara and I were at when we broke up—the thought of how infinitely more painful it would be with Addi sends panic coursing through me.

So, like a cowardly fool, I nod.

She doesn't say anything. Tears start to pool in her eyes, and I want to reach out with a knuckle and wipe them away. I want to wrap my arms around her and make everything better. But then she just turns and walks toward the inn, so I turn toward my house and close the gate separating our yards.

CHAPTER 22

Addison

I SLUMP into the kitchen where my roommates are all still chatting after washing the dinner dishes in the sink, using water we had to heat up on the stove. "Remember when you guys said that you'd be my soft place to land? I need a room full of downy feathers."

Peyton looks from me to the direction of the backyard and back again, her eyebrows drawn close together. "Just from taking out the garbage?" Then, realization seems to dawn on her, and her hands fly to her mouth. "No. No, no, no. Oh my lands, you two didn't just break up, did you?" She races forward and wraps me in a hug. "What happened?"

"I don't know. He just said he couldn't do it anymore."

Timini and Bex join the hug, and I hold the three of them tight for a long moment.

"No more of an explanation than that?" Timini asks.

I shake my head.

"And you didn't demand one?" Bex asks.

I mean, sure, I could have. I just didn't think I could handle the answer.

"Oh my goodness," Peyton says, looking around frantically. "I told you that if you ever broke up, I would provide cake, and I have no cake!"

"It's okay," Bex says, walking over to the freezer. "I think I have fudge pops in here. Yep! A full box." She sets it on the island counter that we've all gravitated toward and tears the box open. She even pulls one out for me, takes off the wrapper, and puts the stick in my hand.

I'm pretty sure I don't want a fudge pop, but I lick it anyway. "My list said not to rush a new relationship, and I swear I didn't. I actually kept myself away from him when I really wanted to see him just to slow it down. I know it's only been ten weeks that I've known him again. It just kind of went fast even without me helping it along. So that makes this my second breakup in just under three months. See? I told you rebound dating was bad."

Timini shakes her head. "Ian wasn't a rebound, and you know it."

I let out a huge sigh. "I know I know it. That's what makes it so awful." I lick my fudge pop and then run a hand across my forehead. "When I first broke up with Matthew, I think what I mourned was the loss of certainty of knowing what the future held, because I no longer knew what my life was going to be like."

I set my fudge pop down on its wrapper. I really don't want to have to keep licking it, and if I don't, it's going to melt all over my hand.

"But with Ian, nothing has been certain, and I had no idea what the future held. The only thing I knew was that I was going to wake up, he was going to be amazing, and I was going to be more in love with him than I was the day before. That was the constant I could count on."

I know that the shock of the sudden breakup isn't over, and when it is, that's when I'm going to feel the full depth of what I've lost. I can feel the weight of it hanging around the periphery, like an actor waiting for his turn to take the stage.

Bex tosses the remainder of her own fudge pop into the garbage can and then puts an arm around me. "Come. Let's go into the gathering room. We'll all squish together on the big couch and either watch music videos of sad breakup songs on YouTube or an action flick on Netflix where the love interest dies. Your choice."

I nod and let them lead me into the gathering room. I'll watch and soak in their support and strength as long as I can until the grief and loss won't wait any longer for their turn on stage. Then I'll flee to the solitude of my bedroom.

CHAPTER 23

Ian

I'M INSTALLING the trim around a doorframe in another new house that Garrett is the general contractor for when he comes to check on everything. As soon as my friend sees my face, he jerks back in surprise. I just grab the board I've already cut for the right side of the door and line it up with one hand, finish nailer in the other.

"Bad night?" Garrett tries to act nonchalant, as if he didn't just notice how awful I look.

"You could say that."

"Have trouble sleeping?"

"Yep."

"Drank a Mountain Dew after eight p.m. again, huh?"

I don't say anything—I just keep nailing.

"Oh. *Oh*. Addison broke up with you, huh? I'm so sorry, man."

"I broke up with her." I grab the stepstool and the piece for the top of the door and start lining it up.

"*You.* The guy who is so in love with a woman that he actually started singing on the job *broke up with her.* Dude, that makes no sense whatsoever."

I just keep working and don't answer.

"It was fear, wasn't it? Ian, you can't let that stop you. It's not right."

"Of course, it's going to stop me. That's fear's entire purpose."

Garrett stays quiet for a few minutes while I grab the three pieces of trim I've cut for the next doorframe and give the air hose a shake to untangle it as I pull it to the next doorway.

"And how did Addison react?"

I lay two of the pieces of trim on the floor and position the third against the doorframe. "She didn't say a word—she just walked away. I think that means she agrees it was time." I position the finish nailer and pull the trigger, the tool making a *pshhhht* sound as it sinks the nail.

"There are a lot of reasons why she might've walked away. Don't assume you know her reason." He pauses for a moment, then asks, "So, do you think you did the right thing?"

With a hand holding the piece of trim against the frame, I close my eyes and let out a slow breath. "Right before I broke up with her? Yeah. Now? I don't know. All I know is that I feel awful."

"Okay, tell me this. How did you feel right after you and Cara broke up?"

How *did* I feel? I try to look back at those first couple of days with the lens of time I have now and really think about it. "Like the future I had planned was taken away from me, I guess." Another *pshhhht* as I sink another nail.

Garrett nods. "And how do you feel after breaking things off with Addison?"

"Like I'd held the most valuable treasure imaginable in my hands, and I just let go. Not only did I lose it, but I left it damaged."

Garrett stays quiet as I shoot the rest of the finish nails into the piece of trim. Then he says, "That might be a clue as to whether or not you did the wrong thing last night." He thumps me twice on the shoulder and then leaves me alone with my thoughts.

CHAPTER 24

Addison

"Ian and I broke up."

Chloe gasps on the other end of the line. I pull over to the side of the road. I'm on my way to work—wishing for the first time that I didn't have my day filled—when I know I can't make it through the day without talking to my sister.

"Oh, no. I am so sorry. How are you?"

I shake my head and look out at the cars passing by me on the highway. "I feel like my heart finally found what it had been searching for all along, and then it was torn away."

"When did this happen? And why?"

"Last night. He didn't say why, and I didn't ask. It was hard enough hearing that he didn't want to date anymore—I didn't think I could handle hearing the why."

"Fear can be a powerful little monster."

"Yeah, it's not the first time it has stopped me."

"I was talking about Ian."

I pause. "Do you really think that fear was his reason?"

"Addison, I saw how much the man adores you. There's no way he broke up because of you."

My exhale of relief comes out as a sob, and I have to force my emotions down so it doesn't ruin my makeup or make me look all red and puffy right before I step into my client's home.

"What are you going to do about it?"

"What *can* I do? A relationship takes two people, and if one of them doesn't want it to continue, then there's nothing the other one can do about it."

Chloe is silent for a long moment before she speaks again. "Okay, from what I've seen, this is how you normally handle relationships. Correct me if I'm wrong with any of it. You meet a guy who you start to like. You flirt as you get to know each other.

"If you get to know him a bit and you still like him, you hope he'll ask you out. And then if you like dating him, you hope the relationship will progress. If you don't like him, you hope he'll break it off. If you do like him and he breaks it off, you hope he'll figure things out and want to get back together.

"If things continue to go wonderfully, you hope he'll propose. You hope the guy will be on the same page and make the choices you would make and feel bad when he doesn't. Does that sound about right?"

"Pretty much. I guess I'm good at hoping."

"Hope is a really important thing, Addison. But it's only half of the equation. The other half is action. To make dreams come true, you have to have both. Have you ever asked a guy out? Been the one to initiate a first kiss? Been the first to say how you feel about him? Tried to work things out after a breakup if you wanted to still be together?"

Chloe already knows the answer to most of those. But I do say in a quiet voice, "I kissed Ian first."

Chloe squeals. "Yes! I knew he was special! Do you love him?"

I nod, even though Chloe can't see me. "I think I started falling in love with him my first day back in Quicksand, and I've fallen a bit more in love with him every single day since then. I imagine I'll keep falling more in love with him every day for the rest of my life."

Chloe lets out a sigh that sounds like a whimper. "That's so beautiful." She sighs again. "Okay, Addison, listen. You moved to Quicksand for a fresh start, right? You were determined to grab that fresh start by the horns and show it who was boss, right?"

"Right."

"You didn't say that with nearly enough conviction, Addison."

I don't hold back. I take a deep breath and shout, "Right!" Who cares if I just yelled so loudly that the dog in the distance is probably barking in response to my shout?

Chloe's smile is evident in her voice. "So, now you need to figure out what you're going to do about it. When you kissed Ian first, you proved to yourself that you can be the one to take action. And you know what you want. Are you willing to fight for it?"

I take a long, deep breath that fills me with determination and bravery. Then, in a voice Chloe could never accuse of not having enough conviction, I say, "Yes. I am."

CHAPTER 25

Ian

I GO STRAIGHT from finishing the trim at the Olson home to working in my shop, hoping the sound of the saws and sanders will drown out my thoughts. Eventually, though, my stomach is what draws me back to the house.

I walk in the back door and find Grandma and Carol sitting at the kitchen table, eating blueberry crisp and ice cream. I lean down and give Grandma a one-armed hug.

"I didn't make dinner," Grandma says, "but there's still mac and cheese casserole in the fridge. And, of course, warm crisp for dessert. Carol and I are just brainstorming options for her home."

"And offering commiseration," Carol adds.

"The place must feel pretty big with Henry gone," I say, putting some casserole on a plate and covering it.

"Yeah. A little too big. I'm not sure how long I'll be able to keep up with it."

I put the plate in the microwave and start it. "Do you need some help?"

Carol smiles and looks like she's about to get out of her seat to come over and squeeze my cheeks like she did when I was little. "You're a gem, Ian. But I need more help than you can give."

I plan to make small talk with the two of them just until my food finishes warming, then I'll escape to my room to eat and shower. But then Grandma tells me, "Sit." So I sit.

"Now," Carol says, "Shirley told me that you and Addison are no longer dating, but she says you haven't told her much about the why. She's your grandma, and since I've been your honorary grandma since you were a toddler, it's time you spill it."

I know that the combined power of Carol and Grandma is impossible to resist when they want information. I can't fight it, so I take a deep breath and let it out slowly. "It was just a bad idea to start dating her in the first place."

They share a look that makes me want to bolt for the microwave—that dings to let me know my food is ready anyway—and then escape to my room. But Grandma senses it and puts her wrinkled hand on my arm. "Stay. Please."

"You love her."

I glance at Carol. It's not a question—she said it like a fact. So I nod.

"So much more than you ever loved Cara. Or anyone before her."

She's so certain that it makes me flinch in surprise. I've talked to Grandma about Addi and she probably told Carol, but I've never talked about Addi specifically to Carol.

"Oh, don't be surprised that I know. You wore your emotions on your sleeve when you were little, and you still do now. It's clear as day how you feel about Addison."

I glance at Grandma, and she adds, "It's true."

Apparently, I don't have a future in playing poker or being a secret agent. "Okay, yes, I do. It's hard *not* to love her, Carol. She's just amazing. She's so talented and smart and supportive. And so fun to be around. She cares about people, has such big dreams, and she is brave enough to go after them. I love being with her."

Grandma gives a single nod. "And she loves you." She also says it like a fact, not a guess.

"You think so?"

My grandma nods. "She's almost as easy to read as you are. We've talked quite a bit while she's been helping me organize, and I watch how she reacts whenever I bring up the subject of you."

The thought causes an aching in my chest that makes me long to be near her. But if she does love me now, that doesn't mean she always will, and that's the biggest problem. "She said she's questioning every decision she made that brought her here. Even dating me."

"Ian." Grandma's voice is soft, and I turn to her. "In every relationship, you'll each question whether the other person is right for you at some point. Asking yourself those questions and figuring out what the answers are is how you assess whether the relationship has staying power. It's a necessary part of the whole process. It doesn't mean that the relationship is doomed to end."

"And," Carol says, pointing a crooked finger at me, "if

you're going to break things off at the first sign of trouble, then you're denying her the freedom to have any emotions that aren't positive. She deserves to feel whatever feelings she has without worrying that it will mean you'll end the relationship."

It feels like a punch to the gut that leaves my head swimming in a fog. Is that what I've done?

"You don't need to be afraid." Grandma's voice is quiet, yet powerful and certain. "Just trust her. Trust that as she asks herself those questions, she'll find the answers." She reaches out and taps me on the chest, right over my heart. "I can tell that all the love you've got for her in here is bursting full. Trust that, not your fears."

"She's right." Carol's statement is as matter-of-fact as when she stated I love Addi. "You trust those fears of yours, and you're going to miss out on the kind of relationship that me and Henry or your grandma and grandpa had. As Shirley said, trust your love."

I lean back in my chair, letting the force of their words sink into me. After a few moments, I say, "Thanks, Grandma and Carol. I really needed to hear that."

"Do you know what else I've been hearing?" Grandma says. "The microwave beeping to let you know your mac and cheese is done."

I chuckle, then get up and give both of them a hug before getting my dinner out of the microwave.

CHAPTER 26

Addison

I PACE back and forth on the grassy shore of Quicksand River, right next to the cove where Ian and I used to play as kids. I shake out my hands and glance back at the shortcut trail we used to take. By the time I got off work, I wanted to go straight to Ian's house or workshop or job site—wherever he was—and tell him how I feel.

Instead, I decide I want to tell him here. In our favorite place. And at some point today, I got the brilliant idea to ask him to come by writing him a cheesy rhyme that will lead him to me, just like I did so many years ago. It wasn't hard to mimic the style of my twelve-year-old self as a twenty-six-year-old—something Professor Rosati wouldn't be surprised by at all.

Now, though, as I wait for Ian to come—and hope it won't be like that time I forgot to mention the direction he should run, or worse, that he doesn't want to come at all—I wonder if this was a terrible idea.

I run over the poem in my head again. Apparently, they're easy to memorize after all. The first time, I wonder if I should've changed any of the wording. I go through it again, wondering if I gave good directions. And I go through it another time, imagining what Ian might be thinking as he reads it.

You said we shouldn't see each other anymore.
Which is hard, since you're my neighbor next door.
But even more impossible is trying to not love you.
Which I can't do, so I hope you'll follow each clue.
Go where we were given the "unplanned" scooter rides.
Jog 400 feet south to where the road divides.
Take the left that leads to our old animal trail.
At each fork, choose the one more traveled and you'll prevail.
Soon, you'll end up at the place I painted on that rock.
And then maybe we can have a little talk.

I shouldn't have ended it by saying we should talk. Nobody likes to hear those words—they sound ominous and bad. Why didn't I think to change that before having Peyton deliver it to Ian? I hope he doesn't think the worst and it makes him not want to come.

I pull out my phone to check the time. Peyton should've dropped off my rhyme at his house twenty-five minutes ago. If I got a note like that, I'd check my hair and makeup, maybe even change clothes. So five minutes there. The drive is about ten minutes to the quasi-trailhead. And then it's at least a fifteen-minute walk to where I am—if he doesn't take the actual trail, which is two miles down from the viewpoint. With all its meandering, it would take much longer.

And that's assuming he was home when Peyton dropped off the note. And that he even wants to come.

I pace some more.

And some more.

Maybe my directions were bad. Maybe I should've chosen a location we've actually been to as adults, like along Chipper Creek Trail where I lost my shoe. Or the park where we watched Bex's nieces and nephews. Or the high school or that restaurant or the viewpoint or the lemonade stand.

Or maybe I should've just knocked on his front door like normal people do instead of leaving a note.

Finally, I decide I didn't give bad directions—he just isn't coming. I'm bending down to pick up my bag when I hear the sound of footsteps through the undergrowth, and I spin around.

Ian emerges from a non-existent path in the trees that isn't the animal trail shortcut or the main trail. He's a dozen feet from me, wearing dark jeans and a light blue t-shirt so similar to the one he wore when I first saw him in the grocery store, with a plaid shirt over it like a jacket. His hair is perfectly tousled, the sun is shining down on him in the clearing, and he has that amused smile on his face that I love so much.

He jerks a thumb over his shoulder. "I might have, uh, made some wrong choices on a couple of those forks in the path. It's been a while."

I smile. "You have a little…" I motion with my hand on

top of my hair, and he reaches up and pulls out a twig that must've hitched a ride during one of those wrong choices.

He drops a backpack I hadn't noticed he'd been wearing to the ground and steps a few feet closer to me. It's strange, seeing this very grown-up, very beautiful man in the same space we spent so much time in as kids so long ago. Except for some minor changes, the place looks largely the same as it always has.

It's the opposite for us, though. We're the ones who've grown and changed. That crush I had on Ian when I was thirteen was a little sapling. Something I thought had withered and died from lack of water over the years but had really just been waiting for its time to grow into something more beautiful.

Or at least I hope it still has a chance to keep growing. Ian looks like he has things he wants to say just as much as I do, but we're both standing awkwardly on the bank of a river, eight feet apart, not talking.

I look at the bend in the river, where the water laps against the small rocks and dirt as it lazily turns back to join the slightly faster-moving water. Then I meet Ian's eyes. "That night, when you said you didn't think we should see each other anymore"—Ian flinches, but I press forward anyway—"I wanted to say how I really felt. But I was afraid to do it because I wasn't sure you felt the same, so I walked away. Kind of like I did when I was thirteen and I gave you that painted stone. Except this time, I didn't run, so obviously, I'm making progress."

Ian chuckles quietly.

I shake out my nervous hands again and then wipe them

on my hips. Maybe I haven't made as much progress as I thought. I force myself to take a few slow breaths to calm my nerves. "But I'm ready now. I'm ready to tell you exactly how I feel."

Maybe I shouldn't have spent so much time writing the rhyme and then worrying about his reaction to it and spent more time figuring out how to say everything that's in my heart.

"You were a big part of everything magical in my summers as a kid, and you're an essential part of everything magical about my life now. I love the way you look out for everyone and the way you make me laugh. I even the way you smell. Which sounds weird, I know, but you smell *really* great. And that smile! Yep—that one right there. I really love that smile.

"I love the way you get me, and how you'll drop anything to help someone in need. Plus, you have really great eyes. Have I mentioned your eyes? Sometimes they make me forget how to think, which sounds like it'd be a bad thing, but it's somehow not. I just… I love your whole heart, Ian. I love you.

"Anyway, I just wanted you to know that I fought off some pretty big fear demons since we talked at the gate, which I'm pretty sure gave me some impressive muscles." I hold up my arm and flex muscles that are anything other than impressive. "And I guess I'm giving up some pretty big insecurities, too."

I figure it's probably time to quit rambling, so I stop talking and just make eye contact with him. Even though I feel so vulnerable after revealing so much, I fight the urge to look back down at the river. I swallow, then say, "I know you had a pretty serious relationship not too long ago, and maybe we started dating too soon. Maybe you need more time, and I'm happy to give it to you. Because I don't want to be your rebound, Ian. I want to be your forever."

Ian meets my eyes for a long moment, and then, in three strides, he's right in front of me, cupping my face in his hands like I'm the most precious thing in the world and he wants to protect me. I look into those blue eyes, made even more vibrant by the early evening sun. Then, without a word, he leans forward, and his lips meet mine with such intensity that I find myself fisting his shirt at his chest, holding him close.

Then his kiss slows, and it feels like he's pouring his whole heart into it, just like I poured out my heart in words. I slide my hands up and entwine them behind his neck, trying to return his kiss with all the words I hadn't managed to get out.

I never want this moment to end. Eventually, though, Ian breaks the kiss and smiles, leaning his forehead against mine, breathing fast.

"So," I breathe, "does this mean you want to start dating again?"

CHAPTER 27

Ian

I LAUGH, happiness from Addi's words filling every single cell in my body. "I never wanted to *stop* dating. I was just battling my own fear demons." I hold up an arm and flex it, just like she did. "Since you gave up some insecurities, I'll give up my own about the future."

"Oh yeah?"

"I was apparently holding onto them so tightly that it's amazing I didn't choke them to death."

"Fears are pretty resilient creatures."

I glance at the water in our little cove that we used to play in so much as kids, and then I look back at Addi. It's a hot day, and she's wearing shorts, which make her legs look incredible. But more importantly, she's not wearing pants. Her shoes are lace-up canvas ones that look like they can handle getting wet and have a much better chance of staying on her feet than the ones she wore at Chipper Creek. I'm wearing jeans—I hadn't thought about the water, just about all the branches and tall weeds along the animal trail we used as a shortcut so long ago.

"What do you say we recreate the scene you painted on that stone?"

"You want to jump in?"

"For old time's sake."

Addi seems like she's all in, so we go to the spot at the edge of the bank before it drops off to the river a foot and a half below, right by the big cedar tree. I wrap my hand in hers, and she looks at me with a grin so wide and so brilliant that I can't help but feel the same joy. Then, holding hands, just like in her painting, we jump into the river, laughing as we land in the water.

I wrap my arms around Addi's waist, and she slides her hands up to rest just behind my neck as the water swirls at our calves, the gurgling rushing sounds of the river moving faster downstream just beyond our cove.

"I remember the water being deeper," Addi says.

"I remember being worried I was going to step in quicksand and get trapped, and you'd have to save me."

Addi chuckles. "Me, too. And I don't remember it being this cold."

"I don't remember being this in love with you."

Her gaze turns from the river to me, and she smiles. "Is this you, admitting that when you were fourteen and I was thirteen, you were kind of in love with me?"

I try to hold back a smile, but I'm not very successful. "If how much I thought about you over the years is any indication, I'd have to admit that I was."

"You thought of me?"

"Every single summer since then, especially when July rolled around. Every family barbecue. Every time I visited my grandma. Every time I saw any directions written down, even if they didn't rhyme. And every time I saw Legos, or flat stones, or a picture of a shallow river, or an empty field, or the Hideaway Inn."

She studies me for a long moment. "And now?"

"Since the day you moved in, I don't think I've gone a whole five minutes without thinking of you."

"And if that's any indication—"

"Then it's a guarantee, Addison Sparks, that I am hopelessly, completely, more entirely in love with you than I thought it was possible to be. You are perfect exactly how you are, and being with you makes me the happiest I've ever been."

She kisses me on the lips, but she's smiling so much it only lasts half a heartbeat. She stays close enough to kiss me for several long moments, though, both of us grinning like it's time for the Fourth of July fireworks.

"Let's get dried off," I say, reaching for her hand again and leading her up to the bank. I grab my backpack from where I dropped it and pull out a blanket, spreading it on the grassy clearing. "I didn't have time to make a meal, obviously, but," I say, dragging out the word as I reach into my bag, "I brought blueberries. I figured going with what restarted all this would make an appropriate start to us dating again."

"You didn't," she says, playfully pushing my shoulder.

I pull back. "Careful. I like this shirt."

Addi laughs a beautiful laugh that comes from her belly and seems to fill my whole soul.

We sit down next to each other on the blanket, our shoulders touching, and our legs outstretched. Addi leans in close enough that I can feel the breath from her whispers. "Also in honor of new beginnings and embarrassing moments, I used Secret's *Va Va Vanilla*–scented deodorant today. What do you think of that?"

I chuckle softly. "I think," I say, looking deeply into her hazel eyes with that rim of sunshiney gold, "that I fall more and more in love with you every single day."

Epilogue
BEX

I SET one of Ian's moving boxes down in Addison's room. As I'm heading back toward the stairs, I open my phone, hold it up with the video camera turned toward me, and push the *Record* button. "Hello, Bexlandians! As promised, today I'm bringing you the very first video in my *Hidden Inn Roomies* segment! I decided to start with the events of today—"

Timini pokes her head into the frame and cuts me off by saying, "—because she wanted to catch us in all our t-shirt and sweat pants-wearing, ponytail-sporting, box-toting glory."

I switch the camera to get a good shot of Timini. "And it is glorious. This is my roommate, Timini. You can call her Tim." Timini waves at the camera, and then I turn the camera to Peyton as she walks up the stairs. "And this is Peyton, but you can call her Pey."

Peyton comes in close to the camera and says, "No, you can't."

Laughing, I whisper to my viewers, "You totally can—it'll just make her twitchy like that. But no, the real reason we are starting this today is that we are getting a new roommate! Our other roommate is Addison, and she is getting married tomorrow."

All three of us squeal.

"As you can see, we are more than a little excited about it. Ian's a great guy, and they are so freaking adorable together. We are moving most of his stuff in today because the two of them are leaving for their honeymoon straight from their reception, and this way, when they come back from their honeymoon, they'll have a place to come home to. Peyton, what do you think about getting a new roommate?"

"I'll admit that at first, I thought it was a little weird to have a guy moving in. It's always been just the four of us girls, and Ian has always been our next-door neighbor. But then Timini pointed out that, hello, this is an inn! For decades, people—mostly couples, even—have been staying here, and the couples didn't even know each other at all. It really is different here than just a regular apartment. And Ian's great, so we're all just excited. For this and the wedding."

"So am I," I say. "They only wanted a small wedding with just family and a few friends—and they specifically said no video. So sorry, Bexlandians! You won't get to see the wedding itself. But here's a sneak peek of me in my bridesmaid dress." I'll add the picture Timini took of me wearing my dress when I edit the video. "Isn't it fabulous? It's why Adds is my new favorite person ever. I will show you a few pics of the wedding itself in my segment next week."

Addison walks from the gathering room to the lobby at the base of the stairs and opens the front door, so the three of us head down the stairs to join her. We've probably spent way too much time slacking at the top of the stairs anyway. The four of us step onto the big wrap-around porch, leaving the front door open behind us like it's been most of the day.

"And this is my roommate, Addison," I tell the camera. "If you can't tell by the glow, she's the bride-to-be."

Addison smiles, waves, and says, "Hi" to the camera. Then her eyes immediately go to the start of the hedgerow that separates the inn from Ian's house. A few seconds later, Ian and a guy I haven't seen before come into view, hefting a heavy-looking dresser.

I turn the camera to Addison just in time to catch her happy sigh. "I can't believe I get to marry that man tomorrow."

"Girl," I say, "you are so joyfully smitten it's practically bursting out of you. I wish I could bottle it and give some to all of my viewers."

"He's just so..." Addison motions to where her future husband carries the dresser down the curved drive in front of the inn, the weight of the dresser showing off his impressive back muscles. "Perfect."

I chuckle quietly. Addison is so clearly blissfully and completely in love that there's no way my viewers are going to miss it. They are going to eat this up. Especially because Ian is putting off the exact same vibes and that man's emotions show on his face as clear as day. I make sure to get a good long shot of him hefting that dresser.

I've been so focused on showing Addison and Ian and

capturing how they feel about each other that I've practically missed the guy who's helping Ian with the dresser. "Hello, Mister Hot Stuff." I zoom in on the guy, who is also displaying some incredible upper body strength, along with a jawline so strong I want to put my hands on his face. The hair is pretty fabulous, too.

"So, who's the tall drink of cool water on a hot day? Please tell me he's single. And that he has an easygoing personality and a soft spot for YouTubers, puppies, and large, noisy families."

"Don't you already have a date for the wedding?" Peyton asks.

I keep the camera on the guy as they come up the front walk. "Yeah, and he's all those things. But we've already gone out twice, and I can tell you he isn't forever material."

Timini bumps her shoulder into mine. "Which makes him exactly your type."

I laugh as I film the two men hefting the dresser up the stairs and through the door.

"His name is Roman Powell," Addison says. "He's Ian's friend from college. He's in town for the wedding."

The guys set the dresser down in the lobby, and Addison immediately wraps her arms around Ian's neck and tells him how impressive it is that he hauled something that heavy over from his house. Then they kiss, even with the camera aimed right at them.

"See what I'm talking about?" I say to my viewers. "Aren't they just the sweetest couple you've ever seen? I may have to put up some sticky notes about PDA-free zones, though."

"I would think you could come up with a more organized way of making house rules than posting sticky notes everywhere," Roman Powell says.

I flip the phone's camera back to me. "Oh. So the wrong type of guy, then." I roll my eyes, knowing my viewers are probably rolling theirs right along with me. I've gotten enough footage for a bit, so I turn off the camera and slide the phone into my pocket.

"After Roman and I get this dresser upstairs," Ian says, gently brushing his knuckles back and forth along Addison's jawline, "I'm going to head back over to my house and help get some of Carol's things moved into my room. That way, when her grandson comes next week to help her move in with my grandma, they'll just have to switch out my bed for hers."

Addison smiles. "Is your grandma excited to get a new roomie?"

Ian shakes his head, chuckling. "They're like twelve-year-olds going to sleep-away camp for the first time. There has been actual squealing and jumping up and down." Then he turns to us. "You'll check in on them every day while we're on our honeymoon?"

"Of course!" I say. I love Ian's grandma. I've only met Carol a few times, but she seems like a pretty awesome lady, too.

Ian nods a thank you to us and turns back to Addison. "Then I'll get showered and meet you at the dinner tonight."

Okay, so I'll admit that I may have ogled Roman Powell as he and Ian worked to get the dresser up the stairs. He might not be the easy-going type I'm looking for, but he is one good-looking man.

Once the two men head back to Ian's house, I gather Addison, Peyton, and Timini into a circle in the lobby, and we all interlock arms. "This is it. The last night that it's just the four of us."

"Can you believe it? I get to marry Ian tomorrow! I thought this day would never get here."

"I can't believe it either," Timini says. "Especially since you were so strongly for the 'No falling in love' pact at the beginning."

"If I had to guess, I wouldn't have picked you to be the first to break it," Peyton says.

Addison smiles. "'*The first*.' So, that means you know I won't be the only one to break it." She pointedly turns her focus in my direction.

I hold up my hands in defense. "Hey, don't look at me! I am *definitely* not going to break the pact." Peyton or Timini might, but it's not going to be me. I am not going to fall in love.

———

Author's note:

I hope you enjoyed reading Addison's and Ian's story! I had so much fun creating this inn full of women entrepreneurs who became such great friends. And I've enjoyed going back to Hidden Inn and spending time with the roomies as they each find their happily ever after. Next up is Bex and Roman—a couple who were an absolute blast to write! The way they banter with each other is so fun, and they just had so much chemistry from the start. I hope you love reading their story, too. Read on for a teeny sneak peek! We are jumping into the middle of Bex's first chapter.

–Meg

———

I grab Nikki's arm. "I can't believe I haven't told you already! I put a poll out to my viewers asking who they wanted me to interview, and I set it up so anyone could add choices to the list. As you can probably guess, the list grew to roughly the length of a CVS receipt in the first couple of hours, but then favorites started rising to the top. Guess who has been on top for the past thirty-six hours? Corbin Shields!"

"Are you kidding me?! Oh, wow, Bex. If you could get him…"

"I know. The guy has so much charisma, so many inter-ests, and he's always willing to put on a show for his fans. If I could get him to agree to it, I think we'd have a good chance at this award."

I grab my laptop that sits on the edge of the desk and pull it toward me, opening it and turning it on. "The last time I checked—which was over four hours ago—one hundred thirty-two thousand viewers voted to have me interview him. Voting closes in five days, and I'm hoping that he has an impressive enough number by then that he won't want to say no."

I log in and bring up the site. Then I just stare at the poll numbers, not comprehending what I'm seeing.

Nikki leans forward, squinting at the screen. "Who is Roman Powell?"

"*No.* No, no, no. How is he in first place?" I refresh the screen, hoping it's a mistake, but he's still in the number one spot. How did this happen? Corbin Shields is now in second place, a full nine thousand votes behind Roman. I run my hands over my face, but it's about as effective at reversing what happened to the votes in the past four hours as rewinding a movie in hopes that it'll end differently.

"Bex!" Nikki says. "Who is Roman Powell?"

"He's one of the groomsmen from Addison and Ian's wedding."

"Oh. The good-looking one who drove you nuts and made the flower girl chuck the flowers?"

"That's the one. Nikki, he can't win! Corbin Shields is so charismatic that not only will we be able to come up with some fun ideas for the interview, but my audience will eat it up. It'll be a win-win for both of us. Roman, though, is a cardboard cutout of a man in a tailored suit with a severe allergy to fun. His idea of an interview probably includes a desk, studio lighting, one camera angle, and zero smiles."

"But *who is he*? How do"—Nikki motions at the screen—"two hundred fourteen thousand of your viewers even know enough about him to vote for him?"

Get *How to Not Fall for the Wrong Guy* to read Bex's and Roman's story!

I know exactly what I want in life—and it's not a guy like Roman Powell.

He's rigid. Rule-following. Uptight. Basically allergic to fun. So, not my type.

But when he's on the cover of *Business Success* as one of the nation's Top 10 Young (and Single) CEOs, my two million subscribers want me to film a peek into his world. I can survive an interview with Mr. Serious for the sake of great content. Easy.

Except… nothing about the interview goes according to plan.

We're talking about an angry deer, an exploding pickleball, a blanket fort that does *not* survive the night, and a dinner ambushed by my exes. Oh, and let's not forget the growing pile of memes from viewers who are suddenly obsessed with us as an "opposites attract" love story.

But this isn't a romcom. It's real life. And in real life, I'm *not* going to fall for the wrong guy.

Right?

If you're into witty banter, chaos, and heaps of chemistry with a big heart, you'll love How to Not Fall for the Wrong Guy.

Start reading

Spies Don't Fall for Their Asset
Spies Don't Fall for Their Rival
Spies Don't Fall for Their Neighbor

Meg Easton is the *USA Today* bestselling author of contemporary romances and romantic comedies with fun, memorable, swoon-worthy characters, and settings you'll want to pack up and move to. She lives at the foot of a mountain with her name on it (or at least one letter of her name) in Utah. She loves gardening, bike riding, baking, swimming before the sun rises, and spending time with her husband and three kids.

She can be found online at www.megeaston.com

Sign up to receive her newsletter and stay up to date with new releases, get exclusive bonus content, and more.

If you liked this book please leave a review. Your review can help other readers find books they might fall in love with.

youtube.com/@megeastonauthor
bookbub.com/authors/meg-easton
instagram.com/megeaston_author
facebook.com/MegEastonBooks
tiktok.com/@megeaston_author